# BEAUTIFUL LUNATIC

Published by:
The Crescendo Group
Quogue, New York

This is a work of fiction. Names, characters, places and incidents either are the product of the author's imagination or are used fictitiously.

Available from www.amazon.com and other retailers.

ISBN: 978-0-9890061-7-0

*Beautiful Lunatic*

is dedicated to

Ron Rosenberg

and

Joseph Immesberger.


This book exists because of their

inspiration and creative support,


and to

James Gregory Kingston

for his editorial and artistic input.


\*\*\*\*


Special thanks to

Donna Lee McGullam,

instructor extraordinaire,

along with my writing group soulmates

from the

Westhampton Writers' Group

# Chapter 1

*How the hell did I get here?* Jack wondered, plastered against the wall of the inside stairwell a few floors above his art gallery in Midtown Manhattan. He was clutching an 18-inch doll that looked exactly like him complete with skinny jeans, a white shirt and navy blazer. Most disturbing was a miniature pistol in the jacket pocket. Everyone else who had received a mini-me doll had been murdered. He could hear someone breathing close by, but there was no place for him to go.

The gun he had stolen from Jill's apartment was gone. He had no idea what his wife had done with it. It didn't matter since he didn't know how to shoot. Despite the fear it had produced, he found himself remembering the first time he wrapped his fingers around the weapon. Thinking about the cold, hard metal drove his mind back to the evening his nightmare began.

*I never should have gone to the bar that night.*

*One month earlier*

"Come on. Let's go," Jonathan said, locking up the art gallery on East 57<sup>th</sup> Street near Madison Avenue.

"I can't," Jack said. "Caroline gets pissed if I'm late for dinner."

"Nothing wrong with talking about your next exhibit with the manager of your business," Jonathan said.

Jack shook his head. "I want to see the kids before they go to bed."

"One drink, while we survey the female clientele. The Downtown Bar and Grill is buzzing after work."

"I don't know. My father-in-law lives near there. I've avoided that place for years," Jack said, focusing on his sneakers as if they could provide an answer.

"So?"

"Maybe."

"Maybe yes or maybe no?"

Jack hesitated. He didn't like to make Caroline angry. He'd been smitten with her since ninth grade. Life together was way beyond good, except for one thing. He was in his late thirties and she was the only woman he ever slept with. From time to time, he wondered what it would be like to have sex with someone else. He'd never stray, or so he believed. He didn't want to end up divorced and lonely like his wife's dad who still pined over her mother.

"I don't want to risk losing Caroline's trust. I love her too much," Jack said.

"We're talking about a God-damn beverage, not an affair. Twenty minutes, or so," Jonathan said, as they walked to a nearby garage to retrieve Jonathan's motorcycle. Jack hesitated, then climbed on the back, not letting his employee know he was nervous to be on a bike in city traffic.

After an uneventful trip despite heavy traffic, they reached Soho, miraculously found a parking spot and entered the pub Jonathan had selected. Shaking from the ride, once inside Jack was relieved to find a seat at the bar where they ordered drinks and settled down. Almost immediately, a dark-haired woman caught his eye. Her black sweater dress showed every curve.

"My God, she's gorgeous," Jack said, nudging Jonathan and gesturing toward the beauty with his chin.

"Yeah," said Jonathan. "Sexy. Anti-relationship, though. A bit weird. Buy her a drink and make sure she sees your ring. She prefers married men."

"How do you know?"

"She told me. She's a regular."

"I'm not buying her a drink. Caroline would not like me to talk to her."

"Caroline's not here."

"Jonathan, you have no scruples."

"Scruples are for married men. I'm still single. Let's decide on the timing of our next exhibition so I can get going."

"We just got here."

"Yeah," Jonathan said. "But I have a dinner date."

"Why did we come here? We could have tied this up at the gallery."

"The only way to have your full attention is to get you away from the office," Jonathan said, between gulps of his beer. "Check your calendar. Can we hold our show a few weeks after the one in London? We can showcase either of our two new contemporary artists, maybe even combine the presentation."

"That works," Jack said, looking at the date on his iphone. "You better start promotions as soon as possible. And I'd like to bring over the manager of my London place. His British accent and organizational skills will be a real boost."

"You mean Oliver? What can he add? I have everything covered or are you losing faith in me?"

"Don't be ridiculous. You've never let me down. At least not yet," Jack said, with a smile. "I'd like to expose him to the friendlier atmosphere in New York and to work with art advisors as well as directly with customers. Besides, since we attract buyers from around the world, it can't hurt to set an international tone."

Jonathan nodded, downed the rest of his beer, checked his watch.

"I'm off," he said. "If you say hello to the girl who keeps eyeing you, make sure to go home soon. I don't want Caroline to blame me for any mishaps."

While Jack sipped his drink, the girl caught him staring at her and walked over. The citrus fragrance of her perfume arrived first.

"Hate 'Gillian,' everyone calls me Jill," she said, sitting on the empty stool, her knees brushing his.

"Everyone calls me Jack," he said, pushing back his fears. "Can I buy you a drink—beer, soda?"

"Hey, Jack, if this works out, we can run up a hill to fetch a pail of water."

He smiled, feeling awkward. She liked bourbon and coke on the rocks with a wedge of lime, the way he did. He thought it oddly coincidental, or was she coming on?

Enduring the crush of the Thursday night bar scene, and only hearing every third word, Jack surprised himself and suggested they get a table in the bar's near-empty backroom restaurant. He didn't see Caroline's father standing at the other end of the bar talking to an attractive, middle-aged woman, but Detective Donald Donaldson saw him.

Sitting face-to-face, Jack was spellbound. The girl's aquamarine eyes felt like a set of magnets. He wasn't sure what to say, so he continued to stare, nodding his head yes, every once in a while. Jill's black, neon green and marine-blue scarf was a perfect artistic pattern. He would have liked to see it on his wife.

Jill dipped her index finger in her drink then touched Jack's lips with the liquid before sucking on her finger. While Jack turned pale, then red, she shined her big eyes toward her diamond-studded Piaget.

"I have a conference call with an extremely nasty warlord in Hong Kong at midnight," she said. "Would you like to come back to my place over on Eleventh Street? You have to be out by eleven forty-five. Every call is via teleconferencing these days and I'll need time

5

to fix the total mess you're going to make of my hair and make-up."

Jack cleared his throat, hoping he understood her intentions correctly.

"What kind of business are you in?" he said.

"Import/export. Are you coming with me?"

Jack thought about his secret elopement with Caroline when they were both at Yale, she in law school and he at the Graduate School of Art. Then he pictured their fancy church wedding three years later. He knew his twin girls were sitting down to eat. Yet here he was, facing Miss Aqua Eyes, about to make the biggest mistake of his life.

His wife didn't need to know. In, out, finished, return to calm. Never again.

"Yes," Jack said, hoping his nervous heart wasn't pounding aloud.

Inside her apartment, he became so tense he feared he wouldn't be able to be himself. He looked around, trying to adjust to the unfamiliar environment. A sparse desk with an open laptop rested in a corner. A bike helmet sat on a black leather couch. Posters rather than interesting art. No books. No family photos. Nothing like the soft pastels his wife had chosen for their home. Tough girl were the only words that popped into his head. Then he froze. Was he supposed to make the first move? While he stood there, Jill wrapped her arms around his neck and kissed him. She took his hand and led him to her bedroom.

Sex was great. The same, yet different. At first, the unfamiliar was exciting, his ego exploding. Then a wrenching guilt set it. He already wished he could turn back the evening, erase the mistake he had made. She lit up a cigarette. He wanted to leave.

They retreated to their respective neutral corners in the bedroom. Jack gathered his clothes. He held the rumpled pile in his arms suddenly too shy to walk naked to the bathroom. Jill kicked pieces of her wardrobe under the bed before gliding to her bureau. She pulled out a pair of tight Carrera jeans, a silk top and gold necklace, her dress-for-success outfit. No need for more. The computer only captured above the waistline.

"Just let yourself out, my Anthony," she said as she went to her desk, leaving him alone in the bedroom.

"I'll be quiet as a church mouse, Cleopatra," Jack said, trying to mimic a similar sing-song response he didn't feel.

# Chapter 2

As soon as Jill moved to the living room, Jack dressed, then craned his head out the bedroom door to hear bits of the conference call. Jill wasn't wearing a headphone so he could make out a few people introducing themselves from different countries. The next words—signed papers, shipments, storm on the horizon—made him shiver.

He slithered from the bedroom, closer to Jill in her cramped place, plastering himself against a wall. He knew he should leave, but he was curious. His brain was on fire. This was no conventional conference call. What the hell did Jordan have to do with England and the US? More perplexing, how was this woman involved with Hong Kong and Macao? Was his night of sex really a plot within a spy novel? He preferred his quiet, normal life.

As he tried to memorize what he heard, his knees buckled. All that training for a marathon and he still had weak knees. He started to sink toward the floor, then steadied himself on a nearby dresser. When his body slid down, he squeezed open a drawer to continue to hold on, allowing his fingers to slip inside. He felt something hard, cold, metal. *Fuck*. This Jill baby had a gun. Sweat formed on his brow. His hands felt clammy. Without thinking, he lifted the gun and slipped it into the pocket of his blazer, surprised it gave him an erection. Above some static, and voices that sounded oddly similar, he could hear bits of the conversation.

*"Chong Lai from Macao. Nothing arrived."*
*"Jill Foster from the USA. That's because we didn't send anything. There are issues."*
*"Ming Cheung from Hong Kong. To be clear, we have issues."*

Stories of Hong Kong versus Macao raced through Jack's photographic mind. It must be delivery of arms from the United States. But why? He refocused on the conference call, noticing that the speakers never mentioned anything specific. Maybe it was drugs. Perhaps it was an ordinary business activity embellished by his over active imagination. At that moment, Jill turned around.

"Hello, Sherlock," she said as she unbuttoned her creamy silk top. You look confused. She let her blouse slip to the floor, got up and took him by the hand to bring him back to her bedroom. He resisted. This would be a second cheat. His guilt shouted once was enough.

Jill didn't seem upset. Instead, she hit him with her proposition. Only then did he begin to understand her interest was not totally sexual.

"I like your fancy art gallery," she said stroking the tight muscles on his abdomen with her finger. "The name, Jack's Gallery, is not original, but what I found on the Internet is impressive. Seems like you have more in

London, Paris and Florence. It makes me want to schedule something."

"When did you have time to go online?" he said, trying to remember if he had fallen asleep during the past few hours.

"Before we met. Your manager, Jonathan, told me all about his wonderful boss. I've been watching you for a while, seeing you chat up women in the park and other places. Rumor has it you have a great family. Most mornings you drop your girls off at school, second grade, right?"

Jack's throat tightened. He'd deal with Jonathan later. Right now, he tried to determine if she intended to buy some art. It didn't matter as long as sex was only the one time and Caroline didn't find out.

"What did you want to schedule?" he said, as the salesman in him popped up.

"Do you travel to all your galleries?"

"Of course."

"Often?"

"As often as needed, especially for new artists' openings. Why? Are you planning to travel with me?"

"No. But I might send things with you. You wouldn't know what's inside each package. Just be the innocent courier."

Jack didn't like the use of the word innocent. More proof something was off. And he didn't want to be a courier. He had no intention of further complicating his life by getting in the middle of whatever this was. By then they were standing on opposite sides of the living room, intimate strangers facing each other."

"Hey, Jill baby, tell me what you're sending overseas."

"The less you know, the better."

"I'd like to help, but I need to stay clean. Can't mess up the international part of my business. Too lucrative."

His eyes began to twitch, a sign he was nervous.

"I'm part of a group, as I'm sure you overheard," she said, while reaching inside her desk to pull out another gun. "It's not up to me to reveal anything."

Jack wanted to walk out the door, then he wondered if both guns were loaded and didn't move.

"Your wife is beautiful," she said, pointing her weapon at him. "Your kids are cute. The photos online look adorable. Actually, I walked by your apartment building and happen to see them outside. One has your dark hair and brown eyes. The other is a blue-eyed blonde, like your wife."

"You know where I live!"

"I told you, I've been watching. You wouldn't want your family to know about us, would you?"

"Your word against mine."

Jill dragged him back to her bedroom, reached to a remote and pushed a button. A copy of their sexual encounter beamed across the ceiling.

Horrified, Jack silently cursed his ego for accepting her overtures and for craving to know that such a good-looking woman was happy to be with him. Suddenly, her gorgeous eyes looked like daggers. Her sexy, raspy voice sounded like a hiss. Flashes of his wife and daughters raced through his mind followed by imagining he shot Jill. Never having held a gun, he wondered how loud a noise that would make.

"Put down the gun, Watson, and tell me what's next," he said.

Jill lowered her weapon.

"You have a major installation opening in London end of the week," she said. "A perfect time for you to take along a little package."

"How do you know my schedule?"

"The Internet. Your gallery is hyping the artist."

"How do I know you won't tell my wife about tonight even if I do cooperate?"

"You don't."

"Which side are you on?" he said, inching away from the bed, moving back to the living room.

"What do you mean?" she said, following him.

"Good or evil? The United States or one of our enemies?"

"You do have a vivid way of thinking," she said, avoiding an answer.

His luck, the first time he cheats and it's with a Mata Hari.

"I notice the bulge in the front of your pants. Could it be that a bit of danger excites you, Romeo? That's not in your file, she said, putting her gun back in the desk draw.

"You're not my Juliet. This game is over," he said, as he turned his back toward her and walked out of the apartment, angry at Jonathan and angrier at himself.

# Chapter 3

Please be asleep. Please be asleep he kept muttering, a mantra that felt like a prayer. It was past 1:00 AM. A quick nod to the doorman and a ride up the elevator went too quickly. He hoped the polished wooden floor in his apartment at One Fifth Avenue wouldn't squeak as he stepped inside.

In the hallway he removed his shoes and jacket, placing them carefully near his feet. Less movement meant less noise with less of a chance of waking his wife. No such luck. Before he took off his shirt and pants, Caroline emerged from their room. Her hands were on her hips, a stance she sometimes took when she was angry at the kids. She looked adorable in her tight pink tank top and lounge pants.

"Where have you been?" she asked, eyeing the Fitbit that had replaced her Cartier watch. "I tried to reach you by phone."

"At the gallery. I shut my phone while reviewing our upcoming installation. You knew that's where I was."

"You were supposed to come home for dinner. I cooked eggplant parm especially for you."

"I'll eat it tomorrow. After work I went to a bar, a pub, I mean a restaurant. I was hungry. I also had a few drinks."

"You could have called. The girls tried to wait up."

She bent down to pick up his clothes.

"Stop. I'll do that later," he said, grabbing her arm.

"You smell like cigarettes. When did restaurants allow smoking again?" she said, as she pulled her arm away.

He reached out to push back a strand of blonde hair that kept falling away from her ponytail onto her cheek. She slapped his hand away.

It annoyed him that she was interrogating him, much like his mother had done when he was a teen and came in past curfew. At the same time, he longed for the simplicity of being grounded and to have everything be forgiven.

"This is the third time this month you've gone out for a drink," she said, continuing to set out the facts in her quiet way, her training as a prosecuting attorney plugging in.

Jack looked at his wife, who had been his teenaged sweetheart, and remembered how she had kicked his ass in the high school debate club. He braced himself for whatever would come next.

"Are you seeing someone?" she said.

The bluntness was jolting. He was the friendly type, talking to strangers at the next table in restaurants or on line at the movies. He thought Caroline liked his outward behavior so she could be her private self. But over the past few months he had become beyond friendly, using his broad smile and cologne-model good looks to approach mothers with babies, women in power suits on their way to or from work and of course, customers in his art gallery. He had become openly flirtatious with every woman within a six-foot radius.

"No, no, no," Jack said, putting his hands in the air and speaking a little too forcefully to be believable.

"We've been together forever. I know when you're lying and I know when you're leaving out bits of the truth. I repeat. Where have you been?"

"I stayed too long at the pub. No big deal. I love you. You're my everything."

He picked up his clothes and walked to their bedroom.

"You sound as emotional as a weather man talking about clouds moving in," she said, trailing behind him.

He shrugged, hanging up his pants and jacket that contained the gun, wishing the night to end.

"Bar... pub... restaurant... It doesn't matter. Jack, I think you want to go to bed with someone else," she said, challenging him despite her gentle tone.

"That's ridiculous."

He wanted to hold her, but was afraid to come too close. He wondered if traces of Jill's perfume lingered on his body. Hugs would not be the best way to keep his secret.

"Do it. Get it over with," she said. "Then we can go on with our lives."

Jack was sure he didn't hear correctly.

"Are you giving me permission to cheat? To have an affair?"

"Not an affair like my father. That implies affection. I don't want you to care about someone else. Just screw and come home. I mean really come home," she said, walking in circles on the side of the bed."

He yearned to tell her he just did, that he was sorry and would never stray again. He wanted to blame Jonathan, though that was unrealistic. Then he hoped to unburden himself, put the night behind him.

"I have to…I have to…I have to…" he said, as he shook his head and moved his hands in the air, unable to find words amidst his abysmal feelings.

"You realize, of course, what you can do, I can do," she said defiantly.

"You want to go to bed with another man?" This was not the conversation he expected when he had tiptoed into the apartment. "Do you have a particular someone in mind?" Men he had seen near his wife flashed across his eyes.

"No." She paused. "Not yet, though I admit I've thought about it. Having sex with someone else, that is."

"I don't want you to," he said, collapsing onto the floor. Then he thought about his own indiscretion just an hour or so ago and dashed into the shower.

If they both had such thoughts, he wondered if there was something deeper that was wrong with their perfect marriage. He had read that sexual fantasies without actions were normal as long as one didn't act upon them. But he did. All he truly desired was to erase what he decided to call The Happening and pretend he was given a one-time pass.

By the time he came to bed, Caroline was asleep. He took a deep breath, grateful the night was closing down. Before he lay back, he turned his phone back on, muted, then noticed a new text.

"Nite, nite, handsome. See you tomorrow."

He typed one word. "NO."

"Oh yes, Napoleon."

"You're not my Josephine."

He erased the texts and tried to go to asleep.

# Chapter 4

It wasn't her birthday. No celebrations were approaching so Caroline wondered why her father summoned her that morning. The day felt special even before he asked her to meet at Aquagrill, an expensive restaurant over on Spring Street in SoHo.

Though she no longer wore her grandmother's pearls, she still lived as if she did. Today, she dressed elegantly in new black palazzo pants and a white silk blouse. Wearing heels made her stand straighter, feel powerful. She needed that, especially after the tumultuous evening with her husband.

Caroline contemplated telling her father about her problems with Jack, then chucked the idea. She didn't want her marriage to sound as shaky as her parents' relationship had been.

When she entered the restaurant, her father was already tucked in at a table in back, facing the door. The golden-orange walls lent a warm glow to his wrinkled face and once blonde hair that was almost all white.

"Hello, gorgeous," he said, getting up to give her a kiss and pull out her chair before the waiter had a chance to do his thing.

*Always taking over. Always in control.*

She was startled to see him nursing a Macallan neat, a drink he usually ordered in the evening, before dinner. Maybe this meeting was about a health issue, a money problem or circumstances she didn't want to hear regarding her mother and father. As a kid she remembered her father traveling while her mom complained she wasn't invited. Now, her mother was the one doing the rejecting while her father tried to win her back.

"Water, wine or something stronger?"

"White wine. I've already decided to have fish."

"I'll order a bottle. How are Carly and Carrie? Bring them next time. I love when they call me DonDon. Makes up for Grandma Donaldson naming me Donald."

Caroline smiled, then checked the menu. Despite her upscale lifestyle, she blanched at the price of the Sancerre he selected. It meant he would charge this personal meal as a business expense. Ever since she passed the bar, she hated such indiscretions. Besides, a private detective did not earn the kind of money to splurge like this. Something important was on the horizon.

"You should try the Mediterranean Branzino," Don said. "They make it with exactly the right amount of olive oil, lemon and herbs. But first you have to have the oysters. They're famous here."

"You sound like a waiter," she said, squelching her annoyance that he was telling her what to choose. "I'll start with a salad, then lamb chops."

"You said you want fish. I just ordered white wine."

"Okay," I'll have the Branzino with a side of sautéed spinach, though I'm sticking to salad as my first course. Seems like you've eaten here before."

"Often."

"It's only a mile or so from my place," she said. "How come you never stop by?"

"Business lunches."

"You could have said hello after."

"A mile in Manhattan is a giant step away, but I'll try next time."

"Promise. Maybe the walk would do you good, tighten you up like the old days."

He nodded. They both knew it was an empty promise.

"So," he said, as their first course was placed in front of them.

"So," she repeated, refusing to allow him to pull out tidbits of her life while he volunteered nothing.

"So," he said again, lifting his glass in a mock toast.

"So," she said, matching his toast by raising her glass of wine. "You first, Daddy.

"Okay, honey," he said, straightening the collar of his pale blue shirt that didn't need adjusting. "Everything okay at home?"

"What do mean?"

"Nothing in particular," he said, remembering Jack at the bar with the raven-haired beauty. "But if Jack ever hurts you in any way, I'll wring his neck—or maybe just break his balls."

"I've always wanted to help solve your mysteries, but you never let me."

"Don't expect rockets to go off. Sometimes this work is electrifying; sometimes boring. I hope your part stays boring," Don said, removing a new phone from his pocket. "I took the liberty of getting you a burner phone to stay in contact. This way, Jack won't know how often we talk."

"Why can't I tell Jack? We share everything."

"Trust me on this, honey. He's so protective he'll want to stop your involvement. At the end of the mission, we'll kill the phone and you can go back to the way things were," he said, his blue eyes drawing her into the world he just described.

"I already tapped this gal's phone. Trouble is, she's tricky. Never says anything that can be incriminating."

Caroline nibbled her spinach. "Maybe there's nothing incriminating."

"That's what we need to find out. Do we have a deal?" he said with his best smile.

Caroline shrugged, teasing her father, while thrilled to finally work with him. "What's this woman's name?"

"Silver Fox refers to her as Jessica. Jessica Fisher. He thinks since she moved to her latest apartment, she goes by Jill Foster."

# Chapter 5

As Jack approached his Upper East Side gallery, he saw Jill headed down Madison Avenue straight for him. She looked hot in her black leather miniskirt and spiked heels. How could he be so attracted to someone who scared him so much?

"You said no more texts so I came to talk in person," she said, without a trace of a smile.

"There's nothing to talk about."

"My gun."

"What gun?"

"Don't play stupid with me. You're out of your league. Way out."

"Jack knew she was right, but was determined not to let her see how terrified he was as they rode the elevator to the third floor. After his shaking hand managed to get the key into the lock, he slipped inside the gallery, tempted to slam the door in her face. She seemed to sense his thought and quickly slipped past him. He ignored her, moving to his rear office to turn on the ceiling-mounted track lighting that brought out the nuances of the works of art.

Once the gallery was illuminated, Jill walked along, surveying what was for sale. She recognized a David Hockney lithograph. Then there was an abstract by Helen Frankenthaler and a contemporary signed poster by another of her favorite artists. There were prints by Warhol and Murakami as well as original oils by emerging new artists the gallery was famous for finding and supporting.

"I like your business," she said picking up an invoice for over $100,000 from a glass-topped table. "Now I understand how you manage your charmed lifestyle."

"This is private property. Get out," Jack said.

"I might want to purchase something."

"You can't afford anything I sell."

"You have no idea what I can afford. Maybe I'll buy out everything here in one swoop."

"Okay, I get it. You have money. Now leave."

"This is a place of business and we have business."

"I'm not taking your package to London, if that's what you mean. I won't say anything to any authorities and you'll leave me alone. Deal?"

"No deal. You won't say anything to anyone and you most certainly will take my package to London."

"How can you be so sure?"

"I think you'll find the experience exciting. By the way, seems that Carrie forgot her lunch today. I saw you bring it to school before work. Good dad. Very impressive."

Jack could feel his back getting damp with sweat. His eyes started twitching.

"You're flying on Thursday from JFK. British Air flight 1517."

"How do you know?"

"You can't begin to fathom what I know about you. I'll meet you there before you check in. You'll carry the package inside your briefcase."

"Will it pass through security?"

"Of course. We're professionals."

"We?"

"My team. You're the only wild card."

"What if my wife drives me to the airport and comes inside to see me off?"

"Do people still do that? I'm sure you can think of something to discourage her. Bet you're skilled at making up stories. One more won't hurt."

"Let's say, hypothetically speaking, I agree. What happens when I get to London?"

"Check into your hotel and wait for instructions. Someone will text you."

"What's inside? Might as well tell me now since I can always open it."

"Not a good idea. The less you know, the better. In case you get caught, that is."

"Caught? Who would want to catch me? For what?"

"That's not important right now. You'll be watched the whole time. Let's say you'll be by yourself, but not really. And if we bump into each other, you don't know me."

"I wish," Jack said in a whisper, but Jill was already out the door.

\*\*\*\*

It was Monday, three days before his trip. Jack cooked pancakes for the girls and offered to take Caroline to a special lunch.

"I can't," she said. "I'm meeting Dad again."

Jack thought it was strange. They went for months without seeing each other then suddenly father and daughter were getting together twice in one week. And they didn't invite him.

He thought about sending his wife roses, though that sometimes went along with guilty behavior. Instead, he babysat while she went to the gym. The next day he walked the girls to school.

"Tell me a knock-knock joke, Daddy," Carly said, while holding her father's hand.

"Knock, knock," said Jack.

"Who's there?" said Carly.

"Banana," said Jack.

"Banana who?" said Carrie, holding her father's other hand.

"Knock, knock," said Jack.

"Who's there?" said Carly.

"Banana," said Jack.

"Banana who?" said Carrie.

"Knock, knock," said Jack.

"Who's there?" said Carly.

"Orange," said Jack.

"Orange who?" both girls said in unison.

"Orange you glad I didn't say banana again?"

Jack scooped up the girls, one in each arm and walked them into their classroom, looking over his shoulder to see if Jill showed up.

"You're so jumpy," Caroline said later while they strolled together in Washington Square Park. "What's going on?"

"I'm concerned about our show in London."

"You always get nervous before opening a new exhibit. I'm sure you'll have a good turn-out with enough sales to cover costs."

"Maybe."

"Do you want me to ask my mother to watch the kids so I can join you?"

"NO!"

"Wow!"

"Sorry, hon. I guess I am jumpy."

As they walked through the arch onto lower Fifth Avenue, Jack spotted Jill ambling in the same direction. She was wearing a cranberry red wig and another black leather miniskirt along with high-heeled black leather boots. All that was missing was a whip and handcuffs.

He held Caroline's hand tightly, staring at his feet. He couldn't help but think about Jill in her black lace lingerie. Then he thought of the gun. Maybe he would take shooting lessons when he came back from Europe. He wondered if Jill carried a loaded pistol and he started to sweat. His knees felt weak and he couldn't come up with a good excuse or reason to tell Caroline why his body was failing.

"You don't look so good," she said, noticing his flushed face and slow pace. "Maybe you should see a doctor before your trip."

"I'm fine. I have to…I have to…I have to…" Then he fainted.

# Chapter 7

Jack decided to pretend he never opened the package. Rewrapping the paper was easy, despite a tiny tear. If asked, he would say his watch caught on it. Resealing the tape was more challenging. A corner piece had lost its stickiness. He used the white string to keep everything together. Just as he finished, someone slipped a message under his door. He ripped it open as fast as he could, hoping it was from Caroline or Oliver, the director of his London gallery. No such luck.

*Go to Footlocker on Oxford Street. Buy a pair of Adidas Ultraboost 20 neon green sneakers. Put them on, then the manager will give you another note.*

Jack raced to the elevator and ran out of the hotel, glad that Oxford Street was close by.

"I need a pair of neon green sneakers, American size 9," he said to the salesman.

"You mean trainers. That would be 8.5 UK size. Let me see what we have left. It's a bloody popular choice today."

The salesman returned carrying a pair of neon green shoelaces.

"So sorry, sir. We sold the last pair in your size a few hours ago. Maybe you can make do with these laces until we get another shipment."

"I need them now," Jack said, practically shouting. The manager came over to see what the commotion was about.

"I do have one pair left," he said, but we're holding them for someone. You wouldn't happen to be Jack, would you?"

"Yes! Yes, I'm Jack."

"Jolly good then. You were supposed to introduce yourself."

The manager bent down to a shelf by the cash register and picked up a box. "I would have given them to you right away."

Jack grabbed the box and changed his shoes.

"How much do I owe you?"

"Nothing, sir. The woman paid. She left you this note. You're all set, mate."

Jack thanked the man, looked in the mirror and felt like a clown. He then tore open the note.

*Go into Hyde Park. Enter through the Marble Arch to the Speaker's Corner. Follow Nicholas Hemingway Walk to the Reformer's Tree. Someone wearing a neon green jacket with a J printed on it will be waiting for you. Give that person the package.*

Jack raced out to the park. Finding the mosaic Reformer's Tree was easy.

He looked around. The park was busy. A group of teenage boys were skateboarding, two wearing neon green trainers. A young mother, dressed in navy blue, was pushing a pram. Obviously, not his contact. Then he passed an old man with grey hair sticking out of his cap. He was wearing a brown tweed blazer and leaning on a walker. Not his contact either.

Two girls, wearing Zara denim neon green jackets, roller-bladed along the path. He was about to approach them when a pair of bobbies, in dark blue uniforms and tall helmets, ambled by. The short clubs and whistles they carried made Jack feel edgy so he let the girls slip by.

Finally, he spotted a young woman in a neon green jacket with a giant J on the front right side. She was sitting alone on a bench. *Nobody could miss such a flashy garment.* For some reason, he had expected to see Jill in another disguise, or a man. Instead, he was face to face with a beautiful blonde whose smile was as radiant as her jacket. She seemed approachable, friendly. It made him feel calm.

"Hello, Jack," she said, in a voice that was too deep for her appearance.

She didn't say enough to hear whether she was British or American.

"I like your sneakers. You are Jack, right?"

*She called them sneakers. Must be American.*

"Right," he said, standing in front of her, trying to smile. "Who are you and what's next?"

"All you need to know is that I'm going to take your package. If we're smart, we'll never see each other again."

"Why not? I bet we could learn a lot about Jill from each other."

"Further contact is not allowed."

"Says who? What kind of ridiculous rules are we following?"

"Don't be a naughty boy, now."

Fuck. She sounded as sexy as she looked. Or was he imagining an upside to this horrendous game? After stepping into a mess with Jill, Jack had promised himself he would never cheat again. He shook his head, as if shaking away any temptation.

"Jill won't like it," the Blonde Girl said, then giggled while removing her jacket to reveal a low-cut, tight t-shirt. "Do we care?"

"How will she know what we say to each other if you don't tell her?"

He leaned close, unaware that the old man in the brown tweed blazer was taking their photo.

"We can whisper in case someone is trailing us and listening in," Jack said.

"Give it to me, Jack."

"What?"

"The package. For God's sake, what did you think I meant? Just give me the package and get out of here."

"I don't know your name. What should I call you?"

"Blonde Girl From The Park."

"That's not a name."

"It is now."

The girl looked at the wrapping. She turned the box around four times.

"You opened it, didn't you? I knew you'd be wicked the moment I saw you."

"Opening a package is not wicked."

"Don't worry. I'll say it was in perfect condition when you gave it to me. I'll tell Jill I dropped it and it tore."

"Why help me?"

"Would you believe it's because I like your smile? Or maybe I miss talking to another American. It doesn't matter. I want to get this over with and go home to my husband knowing I did something right. Let's say this is your lucky day."

Blonde Girl From The Park threw the box on the cement, then kicked it.

"See, you didn't flinch. You know what's inside. You understand there's nothing dangerous—right now. Someday I'm gonna kick one of these packages and it'll blow my foot off."

"Not today," Jack said, sitting beside her.

"You're so predictable."

"Does Jill torture every guy she sleeps with?"

"I bet you never slept with Jill. You might have had some fun, but sleeping is never on her agenda."

"I assume the J on your jacket stands for Jill," Jack said, ignoring the girl's statement.

"Almost. It stands for Jill's SWAT team."

"A SWAT team like special weapons and

tactics? Like highly trained FBI agents ready to free hostages and help fight terrorism?"

"You do have a vivid imagination. Maybe SWAT is wrong. Then, again, maybe it's spot on."

The girl stood. Her skirt was so short her panties were visible as she wiggled by him toward the Princess Diana Memorial.

Jack remained in place, staring at the old man with the walker. There was something familiar about him. Could it be Jill in another disguise? He was tempted to run over and pull off the mustache. If it weren't fake, the bobbies would be on top of him in a flash. Better to keep an eye on the future and focus on the art to be displayed at his gallery. He had done what Jill asked. Game over.

# Chapter 8

Caroline grabbed an outside table at a café near Jill's place on West 11<sup>th</sup> Street. The apartment building was a small brick walk-up surrounded by similar buildings. Despite two trees and some plants, the front steps were visible, enabling her to see everyone coming or going.

She had googled Jill Foster and Gillian Foster. There were many females with that name, but none fit the right age bracket in Manhattan. According to the Internet, that woman didn't exist.

Then she googled Jessica Fisher and found plenty. High school cheerleader, academic awards, lead actress in college plays. Nothing was incriminating. Her efforts felt superficial. Anyone could check the Internet and discover the same information.

Caroline knew she should have told her father where she was going, but she was antsy, anxious to break up her mommy routine. She wanted to do something on her own without being given too much direction.

Finding Jill was her first goal. If she came out, Caroline's plan was to walk with her, trying to be friendly. If some other person emerged, she would try to start a conversation hoping that would reveal something about her neighbor. Any facts were better than nothing.

By the time Caroline finished sipping her second cappuccino, nobody appeared. She felt she was wasting her time. Maybe she could find the girl at home.

Caroline walked across the street. Inside the outer vestibule was a row of mailboxes. One said Foster: 3. She rang a different buzzer at random and waited. No response. She tried another resident. Nothing. Part of her was glad. She wasn't sure what she would say if someone answered. Just then, an old woman opened the heavy wooden door that separated the inner lobby from the street, giving Caroline enough time to slip inside. She glanced around at four apartments on the first floor. The door of number three was wide open.

"Hello," Caroline shouted bending her head inside. "Anyone here?"

She knew she was trespassing and prayed nobody would challenge her. The living room had furniture—a black leather couch, two lounge chairs, a desk and chair. Dust on the desk outlined a clean spot where a computer must have rested. Vacant bookcases lined one wall. She could see two cheaply framed posters hanging above the couch.

The bathroom was bare, not even a towel. The bed in the bedroom had no linen. Two pillows were on the floor. The closet was filled with hangers, but no clothes. Empty drawers were pulled open. She smiled to herself, having fun, then went back into the hallway to call her father.

"Dad, I went to Jill's building to find her. She's gone."

"How do you know?"

"Her apartment's been cleared out. At least I think it's her place. Her door was open so I went in. There's furniture, but nothing personal."

"Are you wearing gloves?"

"No. I was going to watch her, not do a search."

"For God's sake, don't touch anything. I'm coming right over. Wait for me outside. And make sure the door is unlocked."

Caroline stayed in the lobby so she could let her father in. It took him only ten minutes to get there though it felt like over half an hour. He gave her his usual peck on the check.

"Come with me," he said, grabbing her arm and moving toward the unoccupied apartment. "Show me everything."

"There's nothing to show. No food. No garbage. Nothing except for a citrus smell."

"Must be her perfume," Don said. 'If it's still in the air, she left recently."

"Maybe she's here, in the area."

"Could be," Don said as he put on gloves, took photos of each room, then bent down to look under the furniture.

"You're so thorough," Caroline said.

"Score another point for the man without an Ivy League degree."

"Stop it, Dad. We all know you're smart. Actually, I checked under the bed," she said, feeling quite proud. "I found four wrist flash drives in different colors and one thumb drive."

Don nodded. "That's my girl. I'll hold on to them," he said, extending his hand. "They might be the most important part of the case."

"Can I watch them with you?" she said digging into her handbag.

"Me first, honey. Might be a red herring."

"You think she left them on purpose?"

"This girl was careful to remove all signs of life. Could be she wanted us, or someone, to find them."

"This is exciting."

"Surveillance is only exciting in the movies."

"If the small drive turns out to be an audio file, can we listen to it in your car?"

"Now?"

"First, we need to wipe down anything you touched, including the doorknob. Then we can try. I'm parked nearby."

While father and daughter walked down the block, they stared at any young females passing by. A redhead holding a small dog smiled at them. A brunette pushing twins in a double stroller was talking on a phone. The bright sun fueled the friendly atmosphere of the gentle downtown neighborhood, as far away from sinister as an area could be.

Caroline stopped at a motorcycle, a Harley-Davidson. While she admired its black and chrome look, a thin woman in black tights, black leather jacket and black boots approached, seemingly from nowhere. She already had on her helmet and visor.

"Fantastic, isn't it?" the woman said, touching her cycle as if it were a pet.

"I love the sleek lines," Caroline said.

Don started to sniff the air in an exaggerated way.

"Want a ride?" the woman said, as she mounted her bike.

Before Caroline could answer, Don put his hand through his daughter's arm and moved her forward.

"Excuse us," he said, opening his car door that was a few cars in front of the Harley. "We're late for an appointment."

The girl rode off.

"Would you have gone with her?" Don said.

"Of course not. Bikes scare me. And she looks tough. Besides, you always told me not to accept rides from strangers," Caroline said with a laugh.

"This is no time to be funny. That chick is wearing the same perfume we smelled in the apartment. I think it was Jill," Don said. "I couldn't get a good look at her face."

Inside Don's car he turned on the motor, popped the thumb drive into the USB port and leaned back in the driver's seat. There was a tremendous amount of static before they heard a short conversation.

*"Chong Lai from Macao. Nothing arrived."*

*"Jill Foster from the USA. That's because we didn't send anything. There are issues.*

*"Ming Cheung from Hong Kong. To be clear, we have issues."*

The static came on again. The voices repeated the same conversation.

*"Chong Lai from Macao. Nothing arrived."*

*"Jill Foster from the USA. That's because we didn't send anything. There are issues."*

*"Ming Cheung from Hong Kong. To be clear, we have issues.*

"Fuck," Don said. "This is identical to the discussion Silver Fox transcribed for me, only it's repeating itself."

"Is that good?"

"It's not a real conversation."

"Then what is it?"

"A continuous loop. The same exchange over and over. All the voices sound similar, feminine. Most likely Jill created it. I don't know if she shares the tape with others or simply amuses herself by teasing whomever she entices to her apartment."

"What does that mean?" Caroline said.

"It means there's no crime. She can play her recording and move her location as often as she likes. We have no reason to be involved. And Silver Fox doesn't have to alert the FBI."

"So, we're off the case."

"Possibly. I need to view the flash drives before we decide."

# Chapter 9

*Two years earlier*

Before Jill moved to Manhattan, she was Jessica Fisher, a popular girl who suffered from "bestitis." Everything had to be just right. Maybe that was one of the reasons she was pleased to be an only child. Less competition. No comparisons. When her father suggested they go on a trip together, she was glad it would be just the two of them.

"We need to reconnect," Brian said. "Let's go somewhere. What do you think?"

"Maybe," Jessica said, knowing her noncommittal answer would annoy him. Then an idea started to form, a way to complete something she had been thinking about for quite some time. A trip would provide the ideal opportunity to carry out her plan.

"We've enjoyed hiking during holiday breaks," she said. "How about we go out west, to Aspen. We can talk while we do some serious climbing."

"Great idea. It's September so the mountains will be stunning" Brian said, "and the summer crowds will be gone. I hear Maroon Bells-Snowmass Wilderness is beautiful. I hope we can start to heal the rift that's been festering since you graduated from university last year."

Jessica smiled, though reconciling was not part of her scheme. The man who taught her how to ride a bicycle and helped her open a bank account and gave interest free loans to friends and employees, had a devious side. He cheated on her mother. Once she discovered the flaw in her perfect family, Daddy could never be trusted. Yet her mother had stayed.

Perhaps it was their multi-million-dollar home in the Belle Haven section of Greenwich, Connecticut that kept the couple together. Maybe it was simply a desire to pretend their household was still complete. Jessica tried to talk to her mom, asking her if she wanted revenge. Her mother never responded.

Then her mother died. Well, she didn't just die. After learning that Brian kept a mistress for over a year, Linda swallowed an enormous amount of sleeping pills and quietly slipped away. Jessica continued to live in the same house with her father. While he claimed he adored her, she walked around him, hardly talking. It was time for a change.

Jessica bought airline tickets, secured the best seats, rented a Jeep and reserved the St. Regis for their mini break. She studied the trails before deciding which would fit their level of expertise. After packing her old hiking boots, at the last minute, longing for her mother, she included her childhood doll, the one her mother had presented as a special present when she was in grade school. It was supposed to look like her, but the eyes were not light enough; the dark hair, not long enough. The face was the same as thousands of other dolls.

"Mommy, there must be a place that makes dolls that really look like people," she had said. "When I grow up, I'll find that company."

"You'll need money to have a custom-made doll," said her mother.

"I'll marry a rich man like you did."

"Then other women will try to steal him."

"If I earn my own money, will men try to steal me?"

"I doubt it," her mother said. "You'll probably scare them away."

When she grew up, men were not afraid of Jessica. Her beauty attracted them. She knew how to flirt, to be friendly, to dress suggestively while maintaining a classy allure. She used her brainpower to keep the ones she wanted.

In college, she pledged the best sorority and joined the drama club, relishing the make-up and costumes that let her transform into someone else. For this excursion, she planned to take on the role of devoted daughter.

The first day in Aspen, Jessica was irritated. There was none of the promised talk. Instead, her father rested to acclimate to the change of altitude.

In town she bought a Colorado Outdoor Recreation Search and Rescue Card, just in case. She also purchased an Allagash fixed blade hunting knife, charging it to her father's credit card. Full of energy, she explored on her own. The Roaring Fork public bus from downtown Aspen took her to the start of the Maroon

Bells scenic trail. It was filled with other hikers, including kids. Her father could handle it.

The next day, Jessica felt distant from her dad, much like the way they coexisted at home. When they arrived at Maroon Lake, she clicked photos on her iphone, enjoying the emerald green meadows and Aspen trees soaking up sun. Seeing the reflective water with pink sand, two snow-striped mountaintops, and rushing streams were well worth the short break. Meanwhile, Brian lay back in a field of wild flowers, a hat covering his face. After about 15 minutes, she felt ready to let him vent.

"What did you want to talk about?" she said.

Her father sat up and sighed. "It's been a year since Mom passed."

"She didn't pass. She killed herself. Because you cheated."

"You're not making this any easier."

"Making what easier?"

"I've been alone for a year," he said, avoiding eye contact. "I want to marry again."

Jessica was stunned. She had no interest in being handed a stepmother so her father could be happy. Maybe his love interest was the same person he had been seeing when her mother was alive. She didn't dare probe.

"Daddy, do you love me?"

"Don't ask silly questions."

Jessica smirked, feeling a familiar anger boiling up.

"I think you'll like my new bride if you give her a chance."

Though she had many questions, Jessica preferred to pretend her father never told her anything. That would make him uncomfortable.

"Crater Lake's not far from here," she said. "Let's trek over there before we head back."

"I think that trail's too challenging for me. Besides, I have a big surprise. I've been waiting for a special moment to share it," he said.

Brian opened his backpack and removed two 18-inch dolls. One looked exactly like Jessica. The other was a replica of him.

"My goodness!" Jessica said, hugging her doll and almost shrieking. "Where did you get these?"

"I found a place in Manhattan on the West side. Pretty good, huh? Better than the one that disappointed you as a kid."

"You remember how upset I was."

"Of course I remember. I'm your father."

Jessica was filled with mixed emotions. There was a certain amount of comfort to the old doll that carried memories of her mother, yet the new one was far superior. In a creepy way, it looked like her twin. Still, she was touched her dad gave her something so special.

"It's unbelievable," she said. "Why did you give it to me here instead of at home or at the hotel? We'll have to carry it on the mountain."

"I was hoping to make this experience a more memorable bond."

Jessica pushed away any feelings, both good and bad, not allowing impractical sentiments to interfere with her plan.

"Thank you for the doll and the thought," she said tucking it into her backpack. She let him give her a hug, the first in almost a year.

"I'm afraid I'm beat," Brian said. "Are you ready to go back?"

"Soon. There's still one more place I want to show you."

"How far is it?"

"I'm not sure. I don't know if the route I see in the guidebook is the one we're on," she said, not telling her father she had already climbed the trail yesterday and knew exactly where they were.

"You go, sweetheart," he said. "I'll take a nap."

"Don't you want to see Crater Lake? Not the whole loop, but some of it. We can turn around when we get to the stony part."

"Okay. You win, as long as we move slowly."

"No problem, Dad. You set the pace."

Once they passed the Aspen Forest, the second trail turned far steeper, filled with rocks. Brian tripped. Jessica reached out, offering him a hand. A few minutes later, at the most precipitous spot, she stopped and sat between the rocks.

"This isn't a safe place to rest," her father said. "Too near the edge."

"We'll be careful," his daughter said, pulling out a bottle of water from her backpack. "Want some?"

"Sure," he said stepping close and bending down to take the water. At the same time, she stretched out her tired legs.

In one awkward moment he stumbled over her foot and lost his balance, falling onto his hands and knees facing the border of the path, looking down, many feet below.

"I guess I need your help again," he said.

Jessica sprang up, put her arms out, grabbed his belt with one hand while placing her other hand on the back of his shirt as if to bring him to safety. If another climber were watching, it would be hard to tell if she pulled or pushed. While he fell forward on the rocks, tumbling down to the next area, she felt calm.

When he screamed, she shouted. Nobody was close enough to hear them. There was no cell phone service. No way to call for help. As she looked down at her father's body lying upon rocks on a lower level, his neck twisted, she felt her rage slip away. As she watched blood ooze from his face, her father's advice echoed in her brain: *Planning, patience, perfection.* She tossed his doll down to him, then started her journey back.

The death of a hiker was in local papers the next day. The *GreenwichTime* extolled Brian Fisher's career in finance and philanthropy as well as his generosity to friends and neighbors. *Backpacker* and *Outsider* magazines included pictures of the lakes as well as Fisher with his daughter. The sheriff talked to Jessica, but never challenged her, never tried to unravel the many textures to her truths. He should have.

# Chapter 10

Jack raced back to the hotel. The breeze moving through his hair cleared all remnants of the encounter in the park. With every step, he thought of the exhibition that would open in a few hours. His manager, Oliver, had taken care of champagne and hors d'oeuvres, invited the press and wrote descriptions of the artist and his work to distribute to attendees. There was little left to do. By the time he entered the lobby, he felt as if he had regained control of his life. Until he saw his wife.

"Caroline! What are you doing here?"

"Thanks for the welcome. I love you, too. The least you can do is pretend you're glad to see me."

"Of course I'm glad. It's a bit of a surprise, that's all," he said, giving her a kiss on her nose. "Are the kids here, too?"

"Kids are with my mom. Interesting sneakers. You wearing them tonight?"

"Very funny," he said, picking up her luggage. In the elevator, he grabbed her by the waist, giving her a hug and a kiss. "I'm really happy you're here. Perfect timing. Everything is good now."

On the way to his room, he prayed there would be no more surprises.

****

That night, the gallery was popping. Fashionably dressed young women in short skirts paired with ultra-high high heels or black sneakers were done up with pink, orange or blue hair. Some men wore suit jackets. Others wore fitted t-shirts and jeans and sported tattoos on perfectly sculpted arms. The younger attendees seemed more interested in each other than the paintings. Jack didn't mind. It was a happening and he liked the buzz. A six-foot tall woman with a base voice, or maybe it was a man, seemed captivated by three young men. *Late Night Feelings* by Mark Ronson, could be heard softly above the din of the crowd. Some guests spilled onto the sidewalk, carrying glasses of champagne and attracting passersby.

Older couples circled round Henry O'Connor, the newest of a trio of contemporary artists Jack's galleries were featuring. O'Connor's work, suggestive of a combination of Jackson Pollock with a hint of Picasso, was trending in both the UK and America. Jack was thrilled Oliver had found him.

After an interview with *The Daily Mail* and the *Art Review* section of *The Times,* Jack began to relax, loving his wife by his side in her tight black dress. Suddenly, the background music blasted decibels higher, piercing his ears. Except for the music, the gathering became eerily quiet.

"That's never happened before," Jack said.

"Maybe somebody touched it by accident."

"Maybe somebody did it on purpose," Jack said, looking around to see if Jill were among the crowd in disguise.

"That's ridiculous. Why would anyone do that?

"Life has been strange, lately. I'll go adjust the volume."

"I'm going to the bathroom," Caroline said. "I mean the loo."

The minute the music was lowered, everyone could hear a series of earsplitting screams coming from the back of the gallery. Reporters, followed by guests, rushed toward the bathroom. Oliver was in the lead, then stopped abruptly, forming a human shield, trying to turn back the throng. He was soon joined by Jack. Caroline emerged from the loo, her face paler than the white walls.

"Honey, you're shaking. What's wrong?" Jack said, putting his arm around her.

"Jack," she said starting to cry. "Jack," she repeated leaning her head on his shoulder. "There's a girl on the floor in the bathroom."

"What are you talking about?"

"A girl. In the bathroom. I think she's dead."

Caroline burst into loud sobs.

"Maybe she's sick and we can help her," Jack said, while his eyes twitched.

"There are neon green laces around her neck. I think she was murdered," Caroline said, trying to catch her breath. "Strangled."

Jack held his wife as tightly as he could, needing the support as much as she did. He could feel her having trouble breathing. Though his legs buckled, he managed to gain control and avoid collapsing.

"You have to call the police," Caroline said, whimpering.

"No," he said. "No police. We have to make her disappear before the press sees her."

"You're crazy. How would we get her out? She's too dead to walk."

Jack felt light-headed. He wanted to sit down, place his head between his knees to avoid fainting, but knew he had to take charge.

"Did you touch her? Did you touch anything?"

"No," she said. "I'm a prosecuting attorney, remember? You have to come look."

"I don't want to," Jack said.

"Maybe you know her. Or Oliver does. She could be from the art world in London. Besides, we ought to close off the area."

"I have to…I have to…I have to…" Jack said flailing his arms above his head, losing himself in the situation as Oliver scurried closer.

"Oliver, we have a problem," Jack said. "A serious problem. Caroline saw a dead body in the ladies' room. We need to remove it before anyone finds it."

"Too late. I heard your wife tell you and I've already called the Metropolitan Police. They're sending someone from homicide."

"Why didn't you check with me first?"

"I'm not even going to bother to answer that, Jack. The police advised me to lock the door. We're not to let anyone leave. I've been busy keeping everyone up front."

Jack, Oliver and Caroline walked as slowly as they could to the loo. Before they got a good glimpse, Jack knew it was Blonde Girl From The Park. She was scrunched up on her back on the floor near the sink. Neon laces were knotted neatly round her neck that was bruised. Her neon green jacket with the J prominently visible in front, was unzipped. His brown package was clutched in one of her hands. Blonde hair cascaded onto her shoulders. Her tongue was swollen and stuck out. Her eyes were bloodshot.

Next to her lay a doll, like a ventriloquist's dummy, about a foot and a half. It looked exactly like the blonde girl with the same generous bottom lip. It wore a miniature neon green jacket sporting a J in front. Someone had spent a lot of thought and money staging this scene.

Feeling champagne bubbling up from his stomach to his throat, Jack held back the urge to vomit. Instead, he stepped close, touched the end of the laces and picked up the brown package.

"Stop!" Caroline said. "Your fingerprints will be all over those things."

Jack dropped the box, gently stroked the girl's cheek then ran into a stall and puked. In the next stall he found Oliver, also throwing up.

As they came out of the bathroom, reporters were pushing their way inside, snapping photos. Jack could hear them yelling.

"What's in the package?"

"See that doll. Looks just like her."

"Must have happened while we were here."

Jack shook Oliver by the shoulders. "Tell the cops I can be reached at Claridge's," he said, then seized Caroline's hand and pulled her through the back door. They ran down the street to the hotel. The elevators were in use so Jack tugged Caroline to the stairs. She took off her heels to keep up with him. Together they sprinted up five flights.

"I can't breathe," Caroline said, between gulps of air.

"I think we should fly home tomorrow," Jack said, as he moved to the men's room to splash cold water on his face.

"I don't think the police will let you leave."

"I'm not a murderer. I want to go home."

"Running away will make you look guilty of something."

"I don't want to deal with this," he said, walking to the closet to search his jacket for the green neon laces. His pockets were empty.

"You've never shirked your responsibilities. It's your gallery. You must talk to the police."

"I don't want to."

"I heard Oliver gasp when he saw the body. I think he knew the girl," Caroline said. "Do you know her?"

"No. I have no idea who she is."

On the bed was an envelope. Caroline opened it and saw three photos: Jack sitting with Blonde Girl From The Park on a bench, Jack leaning into her, Jack handing her the brown package.

The accompanying typed note contained two words:

*Game on.*

# Chapter 11

"Dad, you have to come to London. Jack's in trouble. Big trouble," Caroline said. "A girl was found dead during his art exhibition. In the bathroom. Strangled with neon green shoelaces and holding a doll or puppet that looks like her and a box Jack touched so his fingerprints are all over it and she was wearing a green neon jacket that matches his sneakers and he says he doesn't know her but someone sent us photos of them together."

"Slow down, honey. I need to hear all this again. One fact at a time."

"Okay. After our last meeting, when Jill Foster raced off on her Harley, I asked Mom to watch the girls and flew to London to be with Jack. It was a surprise."

"I got that much from Mom. Skip to the part where Jack stepped into trouble."

"He didn't exactly step into it. Somebody was murdered in his gallery during the opening."

"Is he the one who discovered her? Did he find the body?"

"No. I did! It was awful. I've never seen a murdered person before. It's sad and disgusting and scary. How can you do this for a living?"

"We'll discuss my career another time. Let's stick to what's going on. Is Jack accused of the murder?"

"No. At least not yet. But he touched everything. His fingerprints are on the box and on the laces around her neck."

"What box?"

"She was holding a small package wrapped in brown paper and it looks like she was strangled with the laces that Jack touched."

"That wasn't smart. He might be accused, or a person of interest. Where is he?"

"At the gallery. He wants to fly home tomorrow."

"I doubt he'll be allowed to leave the country so fast. See if you can keep him calm. I'll call my contacts at Interpol, then fly over as soon as I can, hopefully tomorrow."

As Caroline hung up, someone buzzed her room. She stood frozen in front of the hotel room door. The buzzer sounded again. She looked through the peephole and saw a man in a uniform that matched the ones worn by the staff at the front desk.

"Delivery," he said. "I'll leave it here for you."

She waited over ten minutes, checked the peephole again, then opened the door. On the floor was a slim box, wrapped in white tissue paper with a huge pale blue bow. There was no note so she assumed it was a gift from Jack.

She immediately tore it open and was thrilled to find a gorgeous artsy scarf, mostly marine blue with a smattering of neon on a black background. She changed into a black dress, wrapped the scarf loosely around her neck and hurried to the gallery where she found Oliver and Jack engaged in conversation.

"Where did you get that scarf," Jack said, raising his voice.

"Hello to you, too and hello Oliver. Glad to see you this morning."

Oliver nodded. Jack kept quiet.

"It was delivered to our room. It's gorgeous. Didn't you send it?" Caroline said, moving closer to her husband, about to give him a hug.

"No! Take it off. Now!" he said, backing away, remembering that Jill had worn the exact same one the night they met.

"Why are you in such a panic? It's just a scarf," Caroline said. "I was so happy you bought me something special."

"I'll buy you two scarves as long as you get rid of this one," he said, grabbing it from her neck and tossing it into the trash.

When Jack wasn't looking, Caroline picked up the scarf and stuffed it into her handbag.

"Daddy's coming here tomorrow," she said, hiding her hurt feelings while changing the subject.

"Why?"

"Because I asked him to. You're in trouble and can use his help."

"He isn't licensed to work here, so what can he do?"

"Don't be foolish. Daddy's clever. He'll figure something out. He already told me he's calling his contacts at Interpol." Caroline looked at Oliver then added, "The International Criminal Police Organization."

65

"Are you saying you think I murdered that girl?" Jack said.

"Of course not, but your prints are on the package she was holding."

"Everyone saw me touch it," Jack said, then put his arms around his wife, trying to change the hostile mood.

"We don't know if the police received the photos of you with the girl who was murdered," Caroline said. "Obviously, you knew her."

"I realize it looks incriminating, but I never saw her before."

"So, why were you with her? Why so secretive? I feel like I hardly know you," she said, fighting back tears.

"It's complicated."

"Complicated like you did something bad and don't want to tell me?"

"Very funny," Jack said, avoiding an answer. "I'm asking you to trust me, honey. The only time I've been with her was in the park. Someone was watching and waiting to take those photos. I was set up."

"I told Daddy about them. You better be ready to explain why you met her."

**** 

Back in New York, Don had a chance to watch the flash drives. The first showed a dark-haired woman making love with a young blonde girl. Despite her youthful appearance, Blondie sported a diamond

# Chapter 12

"The victim scratched her assailant," Don said, sitting in a swivel chair in the London gallery's back office. "Cells under her fingernails were sent to the crime lab."

"How do you know?" Jack said.

"My friend, the one I mentioned at Interpol. It helps that I'm an ex-cop and licensed detective. The good news is that nothing matches your DNA."

"I could have told you that," Jack said.

"Your word! We needed scientific proof."

"Does that mean we can leave London?" Caroline said.

"Soon. The estimated time of the murder falls at the beginning of your party. With all the people who saw both of you at the front of the gallery, Jack's got an alibi."

"There's something else you should see, Dad."

"No," Jack said, thinking about the photos of himself in Hyde Park. "If the police don't have copies, they become irrelevant."

"What are you talking about? I gotta be aware of any potential evidence."

Caroline retrieved the photos from her handbag.

"So, you did know the victim," Don said, forcing his voice to sound calm.

"I just met her. I don't even know her name. She wanted me to call her Blonde Girl From The Park."

"Why were you together?"

"Dad, I asked him the same question. All I got was 'it's complicated.'"

Jack looked at his feet, at his wife, back to his feet then to his father-in-law. Oliver grabbed the photos to see what they were talking about.

"I've seen her before," he said. "It sickened me when I saw her in the loo. She came into the gallery a few days ago. Asked when the next exhibition would debut. Wanted an invitation. She had an American accent, if that means anything."

"Everything means something," Don said. "I assume you told her to come to the opening."

"Sure did. She was pretty and friendly."

Don studied the photos more carefully. He recognized the victim immediately. She was the blonde girl who had sex with Jill. The outline to a jigsaw puzzle was beginning to develop. According to the flash drives, Jack also knew Jill, but it wasn't clear if Blondie and Jack knew each other before Jack flew to London. Part of Don did not want to find out how the rest of the puzzle fit together, nor did he want to tell his daughter about her husband's misbehavior. He wondered if Blondie was a second transgression for his son-in-law and he worried Jack's life was at risk.

"Jack, how did you know Blondie?" Don said.

"I didn't. Not really."

"And that means?"

"A woman asked me to give someone a package. Told me the person would be wearing that awful neon green. It didn't sound like a big deal. I thought it would be a guy getting the parcel."

"Looks too cozy to be an initial visit," he said. "If the cops have these, it will delay our departure, especially since you claimed you had no idea who she was."

"I don't feel so good," Caroline said.

"I'll take you back to the hotel," Jack said.

"Hold on a minute. Where were you when the first woman approached you?" Don said. "The one with the parcel?"

"JFK."

"The airport! In New York. Some dame asked you to take a package overseas and you did. That's plain stupid. Why would you do such a thing?"

Jack's eyes twitched as he stood there, looking toward Oliver as if his manager could help him.

"What did she look like?"

"Attractive. Dark hair. Piercing blue eyes."

"Let me get this straight. You, the smart guy with a graduate degree from Yale, Ivy League smart, lets a pretty stranger con you to do something dangerous. Maybe you are stupid. Or maybe you already knew this gal. The description sounds like Jill."

"Dad, stop it," Caroline said, putting her arm through her husband's. He doesn't know about Jill. I wasn't allowed to say anything, remember. Besides, you know Jack's got a soft heart. He likes to be helpful."

71

"Helpful my ass. Where's your lawyer brain?" Don said. "Jack, did you open the package?"

"Yes."

"And…"

"And it was filled with cookies."

"Are you shitting me?"

"It's true. The box was filled with chocolate chip cookies."

"When did this broad tell you where to make your delivery?"

"Later. After I checked into the hotel. I got a message."

"That means she knows where we're staying," Don said. "Was it a written message?"

"Yes."

"I need to see it. Unless you threw it out."

Jack looked at his feet again, then nodded "I tore it and tossed it."

"Dad, do you have any idea who this lady is?"

"Like I said, the description sounds like Jill, the crazy person you and I trailed. And lady is not a word that describes her."

"Jack, if Jill's the woman who gave you the cookies, how do you know her?" said Caroline.

"We'll get to that later," Don said. "I'm so grateful you didn't jump on her motorcycle. She may have murdered Blonde Girl From The Park. Or arranged it. If so, we have a crime and we're back on her case. Now, we need a motive. And evidence."

"There's something else I must tell you," Jack said. "When I checked into the hotel, Jill also checked in. She was dressed like a man."

"She's in our fucking hotel! Did you hear what name she used?" Don said.

"No. I left her at reception and took the lift to my room. Should we change hotels?"

"My guess is she'll find you again. It's better that we know where she is."

"Maybe after the murder she left the UK," Caroline said.

"You could be right. I think she's planning to eradicate my newest client. He already received a look-alike doll."

Don stood up, took out his wallet and abruptly changed the subject.

"As soon as you feel better, I want you to get your hair done," he said, handing Caroline his credit card. "Then go to Harrod's or a local upscale boutique and buy a new outfit. Something sexy. My job is to handle the nutcase. Yours is to remind everyone what a knock-out you are."

Caroline gave her father a hug.

"And Jack," Don said. "While your wife is getting all fancied up, you and I will have time for a long heart-to-heart."

# Chapter 13

"Jack. I've known you since you were in ninth grade," Don said, as they ordered high tea in the art deco foyer of the hotel. "You were a likable kid, though a little too good-looking, if you know what I mean."

Jack nodded with the start of a smile, wishing they were sitting in a pub with a pint instead of this formal environment, dressed in navy blazers and crisp-collared shirts.  They were the only two men alone at a table in a room full of women and families. Don had chosen to meet here so he could see his daughter when she returned from shopping.

"You were a teenager when you came to our house to do homework with Caroline. Made my daughter happy. That's what a father wants, right?"

Jack nodded again, wondering where this conversation was headed.

"You're still young, but you've been together for over twenty years. It's rare that a married couple starts sharing their lives at such a young age."

Jack continued to keep quiet. He assumed there was no way Don could know about his biggest mistake. Or could he?

"I still like you," Don said. "Though with your looks, I bet women flirt with you all the time. It's what you do with those overtures that really counts."

Instead of responding, Jack breathed in the elegance of the room awash in bright lights that captured the shine of the fine bone china. As he looked around at the other people speaking softly against the sound of silverware stirring tea, he vowed to take his wife here tomorrow when they could let themselves get lost in the gentle din. Right now, he needed to focus on his father-in-law.

"Jack," Don said, noticing his son-in-law's distant look. "Where are you?"

"Sorry. I was taking in the ambiance and let my mind wander. Caroline would love this place."

By then an array of finger sandwiches, warm scones and sweet pastries had arrived. The waitress prepared and poured the tea at their table. It was hard to differentiate which man was more uncomfortable.

"We have a complicated situation. Seems like my latest client and your troubles are connected."

"Who's your client? Do I know him?"

"No. It's a guy in New York who asked me to find out about a girl he had sex with."

"Why?"

"Good question. But the bigger question you should have asked is what does his experience have to do with you."

"I was getting to that," Jack said, avoiding eye contact. He took a bite out of a smoked Scottish salmon tea sandwich and waited for Don to continue.

"My client, who I nicknamed Silver Fox, is married. Doesn't want his wife to find out about his, er, dalliance."

"Dalliance. What a funny word," Jack said. "You mean he screwed around once."

"For God's sake, I don't give a fuck what words we use. The man cheated on his wife. I have no idea how many times."

Jack stayed silent.

"Our whole family knows I cheated on Martha," Don said in a whisper, "and she threw me out. Who am I to judge another man's behavior?"

Jack let out a sigh that was almost a whistle.

"He wants to stay with his wife," Don said, "so it's best she not find out."

"Why didn't Silver Fox hire you to investigate the girl before he took her to bed?"

"The guy claims it was a spontaneous liaison. Seems like after their encounter, he overheard a disturbing conversation this dame was having with what appears to be international contacts. Silver Fox thought the woman might be involved with weapons or drugs or classified information."

Jack stopped eating. His eyes twitched while he tried to remain composed, forcing himself to swallow what was in his mouth.

"He asked me to find out if she's a spy or doing some sort of illicit business. If she is, he wants me to go to the authorities. Keep him out of it."

Don watched Jack take deep breaths. In spite of his anger toward his son-in-law, he also felt sorry for him.

"Caroline and I found a thumb drive in the girl's apartment. It's a loop of an unusual conversation, a female voice trying to sound like different people from different countries involved with something clandestine, maybe illegal."

"Is it?"

"Nah. Turns out, it's nothing. A joke she plays on the men she seduces. Gives her an aura of intrigue."

"So, despite what we heard on the recording, there's no international team?"

"Not as far as I see. Maybe she's just kinky. My guess is that she's going to blackmail each partner."

"Blackmail! Oh my God," Jack said, as he spilled his tea. "I never thought of that. I mean, I wouldn't have thought of that. Doesn't she need evidence?"

"I'll get to that later. There's more you should know. The woman is youngish, about ten years younger than Caroline so I asked your beloved to help me out. Trail her. Have a conversation with her neighbors. Find whatever she could."

"No!" Jack yelled. Everyone in the restaurant stopped talking and stared at the two Americans. "You keep my wife out of your messy affairs," he said, practically hissing.

"Too late. She was thrilled to have something to do besides take care of Carrie and Carly."

Jack sat back, shaking his head.

"Seems our target has vanished. Emptied her apartment and left in a hurry. We think we saw her ride off on a motorcycle."

"What makes you think this girl rides a motorcycle?"

"I inadvertently parked in front of her bike. As Caroline and I were leaving her apartment, the dame showed up all in black, already wearing her helmet and visor. At least I think it was her. We couldn't see enough of her face to be sure, though she fits the photo I got from Silver Fox. She asked Caroline if she wanted a ride."

"And?"

"And your wife declined, thank God. The girl's empty apartment and departure was so swift it makes me wonder if she has an accomplice."

"Accomplice to what? What's the crime?"

"Could be none. Or like I said, maybe blackmail. And now, maybe murder."

Don sat back allowing Jack to absorb the ramifications of this news.

"We both know I'm talking about Jill. Here's the deal, my boy. Tell me whatever you know about this girl. From the beginning. From the time I saw you have a drink with her at the Downtown Bar and Grill."

"You saw me?"

"Oh yes. And tell me about the blonde who was found dead in your gallery. I suspect it's all connected."

Jack remained silent contemplating his options.

"Oh, I forgot to mention one important detail," Don said. "Caroline found four flash drive bracelets as well as the thumb drive in Jill's apartment. Like I said, we listened to what was on the thumb drive in the car."

Jack nodded. "What about the flash drives?"

"I kept them."

"What's on them?"

"Encounters with her sex partners. Blonde Girl From The Park is one, Silver Fox is another. There are two more. All her sex partners are wearing wedding bands. Nothing else. Just wedding bands."

"Does Caroline know what's on the flash drives?"

"Not yet. I watched them on my own."

Don slammed his fist on the table, shaking all the dishes, moving in as close to Jack as the table would allow, stopping just short of pulling his son-in-law by the collar.

"If you do it again, I'll twist your nuts so hard you won't have the strength to scream."

Don sat back with a smirk.

"You'll have to figure out how to tell your wife that you know Jill. Caroline's persistent and won't let it rest until you say something."

"Can I have the flash drive?" Jack asked in a barely audible voice.

"It's off limits. At the moment."

# Chapter 14

When Jack, Caroline and Grandpa Don emerged from customs at JFK, the girls raced to their parents. That left Don and Martha facing each other, awkwardly alone in the crowd. Don took the lead, bent over and gave his ex-wife a peck on the cheek. It wasn't the first over the past few years. Usually she backed away, an automatic reflex whenever he invaded her space. This time, she smiled. That's all the encouragement he needed.

"Your hair looks great," he said, looking directly at her.

"Had it done this morning."

"For me?" he said. "You're still a bombshell."

Martha smiled, returning his stare.

"I'm also trying out this new outfit I bought now that I'm teaching nutrition. I'm hoping my co instructor will ask me to join him once a week all semester. Do you like it?" she said, twirling like a teenager.

"No."

"No. That's pretty abrupt," she said.

"It's too elegant and sexy at the same time. And the heels are too high. They make you look like a model."

"I'm a grandmother, though flattery is much appreciated."

"Is this Steve guy married?"

"I don't know anything about his personal life. Yet."

"It might give him the wrong idea. Better to wear an old, big dress."

"Why Donald Donaldson, I do believe you're jealous."

Don broke their eye contact, turning toward the twins who were screaming and crying. Carrie had her hand in her mouth, licking a wound her sister had inflicted.

"Carly, why did you bite your sister? That hurts," Don said.

"She took my book and won't give it back."

"Did not," said Carrie.

"Did too."

"I have your book, Carly," Caroline said. "Apologize to her. Right now. You have to stop biting. It's not nice."

Everyone stood around, silently watching the girls make up and hug. Don took this moment to bark out directions, taking over as usual.

"The four of you take one cab," he said to Caroline. "I'll go with Grandma in another."

He opted to ignore the look his daughter exchanged with Jack. Caroline opened her mouth to say something. Jack shook his head and she remained silent, as if it were normal for her parents to be together.

Seated close to Martha in the taxi, Don became emboldened.

"How about I buy you dinner tonight?" he said, leaning toward her, almost whispering the invitation in her ear. "You're all dressed up and ready to go."

"That's so sweet."

"Sweet, but…"

"But I'm tired. The kids knocked me out."

"That's why you deserve a quiet, relaxing meal. No cooking. No dishes."

"Not this time," Martha said.

"It's never the right time."

Martha shrugged. "Besides, your favorite bar and grill is closed. You'd have to try someplace else. I know how much you hate anything new."

"I've only been gone a few days. Why are they closed?"

"A body was found in the back of the restaurant. According to the newspapers, the owner tried to convince the police it was a heart attack or some other natural cause. Anything not to scare away their customers."

"The cops closed the place. Do you know why?"

"Crazy things were discovered. Reading about them made me tremble."

"Like what?"

"First, there was a neon shoelace around the guy's neck."

Don moved away from Martha, suddenly alert. "Was he strangled?"

"How did you guess? I think it would be impossible to strangle someone at a table in a restaurant filled with other diners."

"One would assume so. Especially if he were with someone else."

"That's the most outrageous part. Seated opposite him was a doll that was identical to him. A photo in the paper showed it was dressed like him as well."

Don bent forward. "Take me to the Downtown Bar and Grill over on Greenwich Street," he shouted to the driver. "Then you can drive my wife home."

"I'm not your wife," Martha said.

Don overlooked the comment. "Listen, there was a dead girl found in Jack's gallery in London. Jack was a person of interest. I was able to prove there wasn't enough reason to hold him, though the crime hasn't been solved. We have no motive and no evidence."

"I know. Caroline told me. She also said the victim was called Blonde Girl From The Park and she scratched her murderer. Isn't that evidence?"

"Not definitive enough. We think a broad named Jill is the killer, but even if they get her DNA and it's a match with the skin under Blondie's nails, we don't know for sure that Jill was scratched at the time of the murder. The victim and Jill knew each other."

"What does all this have to do with the dead man in the bar and grill?"

"Everything. The girl in Jack's gallery was clutching a doll that was identical to her. Matching faces. Same outfit. The killings are similar. Have to be connected."

Martha nodded, mulling over the information.

"I think you're right, honey," she said.

"Honey! We're making progress."

"Don't get excited. It was a slip from the past."

"If I can solve this one, I bet I can help Jack," Don said, ignoring his wife's explanation. "The murders were well planned. First, the killer spent time and money to have the dolls made. Lots of money. Then the assassin had to know the victim's routine."

"What are you going to do now?" Martha said.

"I'm taking on the case. After I check out the restaurant, I intend to find out who made the dolls. There can't be that many places."

"Oh, you'd be surprised."

"What are you talking about?"

"My friend decided to make a plush doll out of her granddaughter's drawings. It sounded so good, I looked it up on the Internet. There are lots of companies that do this. Most charge under $100. You also can create a doll that resembles a photo or person."

"The dolls Jill had made probably cost ten times what you quoted."

"Why don't you look up where movies have their props made."

"Honeybunch, you were always clever. That's one of the reasons I fell in love with you."

Martha shook her head and rolled her eyes. "Click on your computer and you can be just as clever."

"Want to work with me on this?" he said.

"Like old times?"

He nodded.

"Be my sounding board again. It'll be fun."

"You've developed an odd sense of fun," Martha said.

By now they had arrived at the Downtown Bar and Grill. He paid then jumped out of the cab as Martha's phone buzzed. It was Steve.

# Chapter 15

Don tried to slip under the crime scene tape that blocked the doorway. A man in a police uniform put up his hand to stop him.

"Sorry, sir. You can't go in here right now."

"I'm Detective Don Donaldson," he said showing his I.D. "Used to be a cop, maybe at your precinct. Who's handling this case?"

"Smith. He's inside talking to the owner."

"Good stroke of luck. He's a friend of mine," Don said.

"Hey, Smith. It's me, Don Donaldson," he shouted, banging on the restaurant door and attracting attention of people walking by. "I have information that'll help you solve this case."

In a nano second, Smith opened the door a crack to see who it was. Don pushed his way inside almost knocking over his friend who was tall, but lanky and stronger than he appeared.

"Long time no see, pal. I've been out of town for a few days. What happened here?" Don said, as they both recovered their balance and strode to the back of the restaurant where Anthony, the owner, was talking to another cop.

"Hello Don. I'm glad to see a familiar face," said Anthony, who was dressed in all black to match his dark hair. Usually, his speech was smooth, pure liquid gold. Right now, he sounded more staccato than velvet. "I can't believe some guy got knocked off in the middle of dinner."

"Did you know him?"

"He was a regular, same as you. Well-dressed, like a big shot at a financial company. Came in a couple of times with his wife. Matching wedding bands, called her The Missus. She was a gorgeous ex-model. They sat opposite each other. Seemed content. Then, every Wednesday night he showed up with a different woman. Turns out, he was a player."

"No shit."

"Always sat next to the girl, his hand on her leg."

"Who was he with when he was murdered?"

"A dummy."

"A stupid broad?"

"A real dummy, like for a ventriloquist, only it was a doll."

Don's stomach heaved.

"Like for Edgar Bergen or Paul Winchell?"

"You're showing your age, Don," said Smith.

"I loved Jerry Mahoney."

"Yeah, well this dummy looked exactly like the guy," said Anthony. "A perfect replica. Probably cost a bundle. First, the man held the dummy, moved its eyes and mouth. Both were handsome. Both had silver hair and wore the same clothes. Even the tiny shoes matched the man's black brogues. Looked expensive. The man seemed to be enjoying his little act while everyone around him stared."

"Silver hair?"

"Yes."

Don shook his head, then faced Smith.

"What's the guy's name? Do you have a photo? I think he was my latest client. If he is, I'm pretty sure who the killer is."

"Well, well, the fabulous Don might just do it again. The man's name is Bill Turner. I'll give you anything else we have as long as you share what you've got."

Anthony stepped between the two and put his arm around Don, clearly showing where his allegiance rested. "There's more. The guy sat the doll across from him."

"Only in New York," Don said.

"He ordered two drinks. Checked the menu then requested two different meals. I indulged him, planning to charge for both. If he wants to toss his money around, who am I to say no. Eventually, the other customers went back to eating their dinners."

"Are you telling me that while so many people were watching, someone walked over and strangled him, yet nobody saw it happen?" Smith said.

"It was early. Place was more than half empty. The man was in a booth in back," said Anthony. "It's dark. Look at the burgundy leather seating, mahogany wood table, dark walls and subtle lighting. The atmosphere enhances a nice shot of bourbon or scotch, a rare steak and an expensive red wine."

"They could still be seen," said Smith.

"Somebody must have hidden behind his seat, reached up with the shoelaces and pulled them tight. Nobody reacted," Anthony said, insisting it was done quietly.

"People kick. They struggle, make noise. They use their hands against their assailant. How quiet could it have been?" Don said.

"We're checking to see if he was drugged," said Smith. "Most likely, something was slipped into his drink. It happened before the main course was served."

"I want to talk to all the waitresses and I need a list of the people who sat nearby.

"For you, Don, I'll give you what I gave the police," Anthony said, looking at Smith to check that it was okay.

"Is there a back door the killer could have used to escape unnoticed?"

"Not nearby."

"Someone could have picked up an apron, dressed like your wait-staff and gone unnoticed to the kitchen," Don said. "My killer likes to do that, put on different costumes, pretend to be someone else. She's good at it. Did she take the dummy?"

"We have it," Smith said. "You curious 'cause of Anthony or are you working this case?"

"I'm working the case as of now."

"I figured as much," said Smith. "The guy's wife is coming to the morgue to identify him. You might as well join us."

"Please don't tell the lady that her husband was my client. He hired me to investigate a woman he took to bed. Our business relationship was just between the two of us. I'd like to honor that even though he's dead."

"My guess is she knew what he was up to and opted to keep quiet."

"Could be," Don said. "Wouldn't be the first time a wife did that. I also need to see the dummy. Maybe there's a label. Once I find out where it was made, I can prove who ordered it and maybe connect our key suspect to the crimes, though that's not enough evidence to convict."

# Chapter 16

As Martha was about to leave the nearby high school, her co-instructor, a Phys. Ed. teacher, known to the students as Mr. Pumped due to his buff body, followed her outside.

"Martha, thanks for helping with the health and nutrition class. Nothing like a skilled nurse to cover the important biological stuff."

"Why Mr. Andrews, it's so nice to be appreciated," she said, while feeling her face turn red. "Since I retired, I miss interaction with people. I'm so glad you found me."

"Your photo on the Internet was even better than your qualifications, and those were perfect."

"I hope you call on me again," she said, blushing. "It was such fun."

"That's exactly what I intend to do," he said, pushing aside whatever gray hair he had left on his balding head, leaning in toward her and lowering his voice. "Call me Steve. It feels less formal."

Martha nodded, stepping back, uncomfortable, yet pleased that he seemed to be flirting with her, or was it her imagination?

She was wearing the same new outfit she had on when she brought the twins to greet their parents at the airport. Standing for an hour in high heels made her feet hurt, but she didn't care. It was good to be elegant once in a while, even if the class was filled with sloppy students who may or may not have been listening to her lecture.

"Maybe we can grab a drink or bite to eat sometime," Steve said, moving closer.

This was the second time a man asked her out to eat while she wore her new suit. She wondered if she looked hungry or if most men considered dinner foreplay.

Martha had not gone out with anyone since she and Don split. After all the years, she was still a one-man woman. Though Don was no longer her husband, her heart had no intention of replacing him. Looking at Steve, she floundered, trying to think of clever banter.

"You're a Phys. Ed. teacher, so for a minute I was worried you were going to invite me to work out at the gym," she said, playing with her hair, glad she had been to the salon to touch up her roots.

"That would be great. I used to exercise with my late wife before she got sick. I'd love the company. Are you interested?"

"Mr. Andrews," she said, beginning to answer.

"Steve," he said, interrupting her.

"Steve, I sure am flattered, but the gym and I are not on the best of terms. I didn't mean to give you the wrong impression. About working out, that is."

Martha cursed herself for sounding so unsure, certain even the sloppy young students could teach her a bit about male-female interactions. She had no problem talking to Don. At her age, she should be able to conduct a better conversation with a colleague.

Steve lowered his head as they stood in silence. She sensed the man's loneliness and felt pity more than anything else. She wondered how long ago his spouse had passed away and if he were ready to be with someone else. Though she didn't want to go out with him, maybe she could introduce him to one of her single friends, someone who liked to work out as much as she liked to cook. A few other nurses popped into her mind and she promised herself to see if they would be interested.

At that moment, students started to pour out of the building. Most carried backpacks. Others clutched a few books. A few girls, in torn jeans and denim jackets or sweaters walked together, eyeing the young boys who seemed uninterested.

"Martha, which way are you going?" Steve said. "Perhaps we can walk together."

"I was going to get some ice cream a block or so from here. You can join me, if you want. They have some amazing flavors, like cinnamon and cherry brandy chocolate, or are you a vanilla person like my ex?"

"Actually, I don't eat ice cream. Too much sugar. There are healthier ways to get a cold treat."

"Really. Like what?"

"Like dairy free frozen treats. Tofutti Cuties have no milk or butter."

Whatever weakness Martha had felt leading her to consider this man's invitation to spend more time together evaporated the moment he suggested no cream ice cream. She questioned if he really approved of her part of the school lecture.

"There are lots of subjects I hope you will cover to make sure the kids understand a balanced diet can taste good," he said. "So many just want chips, French fries, cheeseburgers and cokes. Some are already addicted to coffee, or other Starbuck's drinks."

"What drinks, besides water and juice do you want me to endorse?"

"It's not a matter of endorsement. It's about factual information. You can bring in alternative nutritional studies. Take kale, for instance. It's great for juicing with other greens. I'll bring some for you to taste next week."

"I'm afraid to tell you, I prefer water."

"But you'll try it, right?"

"Not sure. I'm happy with water."

"But if I take the time to prepare it for you, you'll at least taste it."

Martha couldn't decide if she wanted to scream or punch him.

"Looks like while you're teaching about health," he said, "I can clarify some other things about better eating—information that wasn't in textbooks years ago."

"Could be," she said, watching two sets of couples strolling together. One student was holding his girlfriend's books. It made Martha smile. Another two teens were holding hands. Martha couldn't stop watching them, remembering the last time she held Don's hand years ago. She yearned for such a simple gesture of togetherness, only not with Mr. Pumped.

As she walked away from the school, she planned to make her mother's best lasagna and give some to Steve. She'd make it with fake cheese and no meat and wouldn't invite him to eat with her, just give it to him in a take-out plastic tub that he could heat up at home. For sure, she'd cook some with real cheese and sausage for Don. It used to be his favorite dish, with a glass of fine red wine.

# Chapter 17

*One year earlier*

Sex was easy to find. Jessica's financial portfolio was bulging thanks to a small fortune her parents had left in addition to their pricey mini-mansion. She didn't intend to have kids. There was no reason to marry. Ever. Most important of all, if she didn't commit to one man, there would be no worry about infidelity like her mother had faced.

Then there was the blue-eyed, sandy-haired guy next door, wholesome enough to be in a milk commercial. Following her father's death in Colorado, Eddie Halleron stepped up, providing a shoulder to lean on. It was surprisingly comfortable.

"I have a confession to make," she said one evening as they were about to share a glass of Knob Creek bourbon and a lavender bubble bath in the jacuzzi in the master bathroom. "When you're not with me, I keep thinking about my oversized house. While growing up, I was never afraid. Now, I'm scared to be alone. If an intruder comes in, nobody would hear me scream."

She wasn't really afraid. She hoped showing a false vulnerability might encourage Eddie to spend more time in her seven-bedroom house.

"Do you want to move in?" she said.

"Not unless we're married."

"Is that a proposal? No marriage for me."

Eddie didn't seem upset, so he probably wasn't proposing, which was a good thing, because if she ever did accept an invitation to marry, it had to be unique, or extremely romantic.

"Okay," he said. "Here's a deal instead. How about you take private shooting lessons at Stamford Firearm Training. I'll join you. It'll give us more time together."

At first, Jessica was stunned, then amused by the absurd suggestion.

"Might as well," she said. "I think I'd like to own a cute little pistol. Do they come in colors?"

Jessica had a lot of patience so she didn't mind waiting months to get permits. During that period, Eddie was happy to spend more and more evenings at her house. One night a week, they went to fire their guns. Following each lesson, they brought home dinner from different local restaurants then relaxed with a lavender bubble bath. At least once every four weeks, he asked her to marry him. Over time, she began to trust him. Still, it took a year for Jessica to agree to wed.

"I want to make a trade," Eddie said. "Give me your pistol and I'll give you what's inside this box. If you accept, you won't need the gun."

Of course, Jessica understood what was going on. She played along, pretending to be surprised, putting her gun on a table and opening his gift.

"This ring is gorgeous," she said, "exactly what I would have chosen."

Eddie's smile was huge. Surely, they were in sync.

"Now, I have a request," she said. "Can we elope? It'll be so much easier for me, since I don't have my mom."

"I understand," he said, enveloping her in his arms. "Though you do realize that my mother won't hear of it. She'll handle everything."

"Did you discuss this with her already?"

"Um, well, yes."

"How dare your mother orchestrate how we get married!" Jessica said, annoyed at the loss of control.

Seeing Eddie's hurt expression, she backed off. Becoming Mrs. Edward Halleron would give her a new name and new identity, something she had wanted since her trip to Colorado. She decided to take on the role of devoted daughter-in-law and accept his mother's arrangements.

The Belle Haven Yacht Club was perfect, as was the weather. Jessica found herself enjoying every minute of the celebration until the wedding cake was wheeled out. Atop the cake was a ceramic bride and groom, looking as hideous as possible. It reminded Jessica of the generic doll her mother had bought her as a kid, the one she never liked. One model fits all never worked for her. Rather than save this ugly figurine as a souvenir of their wedding, she decided to order a look-alike doll for her new husband. It could sit on a shelf in the den next to the one her father had bought her. *The dolls will be our keepsake until death do us part.*

During their first year of marriage, Eddie commuted to Manhattan, working downtown for JP Morgan Chase. Jessica redecorated, changing her mother's floral everything to more neutral, solid colors. Since she didn't need to work, she explored volunteer opportunities at the Bruce Museum and the local YWCA. Wednesday nights were her bridge nights while Eddie stayed late at the office. Their life was easy until the appearance of the ultimate marital-breaking cliché— lipstick on Eddie's collar.

*Eddie would never cheat. No way.* But the lipstick didn't match Jessica's shade. Not even close.

"Do you have a girlfriend?" Jessica said, while her husband stood, head down as if ready to be slapped.

"No."

So why is there lipstick on your collar?" she said, then raced to their bedroom to check his other shirts.

Eddie followed, mumbling something about not knowing how the stain got there.

"Why is there lipstick here?" she said again, pushing the shirt close to his face.

"It was just a kiss. She initiated it. I had nothing to do with it."

"Who's She? And how can you claim to have nothing to do with it?"

"Some assistant at the office. I don't even know her name. She always asked me to call her Blonde Girl."

"Did you fuck her?"

"Me?"

99

"Who else is standing here?"

He gave a half nod, looking down at his feet.

"Is that a yes or a no?"

"Once. Only once. In the office. She threw herself at me. It was more awkward than good, like when you and I joined the mile-high club in the Delta airplane bathroom."

"Please spare me the details! I suppose you think once makes it okay."

"No. Of course not. It won't happen again. I promise. Never again."

Jessica was enraged. Despite all her caution, her marriage wasn't ideal.

"You're damn right it won't happen again. Unless you intend to pack up and get out. You can go back to next door and have your mother organize your life like she did our wedding."

Anger flared up for herself, for her mother and for all the stupid women who knew what was going on and stayed with their double-dealing spouses. Jessica vowed to handle the situation differently.

First, she needed time to create a flawless plan. Her brain swung from one scenario to another. She still had the knife she had bought in Aspen. But Eddie was strong. To use it, he had to be knocked out first. Besides, stabbings were messy and would leave a lot to explain to the police. Using her gun would cause similar problems. It was important that her husband's demise appear accidental, like her father's.

Jessica decided to approach her problem in stages. She would take on the role of forgiving wife, have sex and fake pleasure to keep him involved. Ideally, she would kill her husband and blame his new lover, except she had no idea who Blonde Girl was.

They continued their weekly bourbon and lavender bubble baths. He filled the tub. She filled their glasses. On the evening of his execution, Jessica started with two crystal tumblers, each containing an inch of alcohol. As expected, Eddie finished his off swiftly and asked for a refill. She took his glass and set it alongside hers in the kitchen for the police to discover.

After filling another tumbler with more bourbon, she added an overdose of his sleeping pills he sometimes used to relax. As soon as they dissolved, she handed him his drink and opened Spotify on her phone, then selected Engelbert Humperdinck singing *The Last Waltz*, the same music her mother had on when she committed suicide.

Jessica climbed into the other end of the tub facing her husband and played with his toes while he sipped the bourbon. She had researched unexpected deaths and knew exactly what to do next.

"Can't we listen to something more up to date?" he said with a slur before dozing.

Jessica looked at her handsome husband, lying in the bath with his eyes closed, his dark blond hair surrounded by bubbles. He appeared peaceful. She placed her hands on his ankles and pulled until his head was under the water. She thought she heard a gurgling sound, but the music was loud so she wasn't sure. Her only regret was that he was dead, making it impossible to kill him again.

She stepped out of the tub, wrapped herself in an oversized white towel, then propped Eddie back up, leaving him in the now tepid water. While eating a light dinner she thought about fetching his look-alike doll to set next to the tub. *Not a good idea. The police might think it weird and ask too many questions.* She left the doll in the den, then crawled into her bed for the rest of the night.

Her scheme was to pretend to discover Eddie in the tub in the morning and take on the role of hysterical widow. They were too young to have looked into wills and she already owned the house so there was no financial benefit for her from his death. If the authorities found traces of sleeping pills in his body, she'd explain that Eddie often took them on his own.

She called the police, confident there was no way she would be found guilty. Her mind wandered back to her childhood, hearing her father teaching her: *Planning, patience, perfection.*

Following the investigation, Jessica intended to move to Manhattan. She'd decide about selling the house she grew up in later. Since she had inherited a small fortune, she could afford two residences without dipping into her stock portfolio. She smiled, thinking there were perks to being a widow and an orphan.

# Chapter 18

Don grabbed a bottle of red from his wine cooler, stopped at a florist to pick up a dozen red roses and continued walking a few blocks north. It was hard to fathom that Martha invited him to dinner and he wasn't going to screw it up.

In front of her door, he adjusted the collar under his newest blue sweater and took a deep breath. He rang her bell while keeping the flowers behind his back, much like he had seen in numerous romantic movies, then counted the footsteps he could hear as she walked to greet him.

"Hello, sweetheart," he said when she opened the door.

"I'm not your sweetheart. And here's your dinner," she said, smiling to soften her words while practically shoving a plastic container of lasagna and another container with salad into him. Then she noticed his hands were full.

"Roses! For me. That's so nice," she said, with genuine good feelings.

She put Don's portable dinner on a side table near the couch and went to get a vase, leaving him standing in the hallway.

"It's okay that I come in, right?" he said, moving further inside and closing the door. The table was set with one place setting and one wine glass.

"Aren't we going to eat together?" he said, rather bewildered.

"That setting is for me. Your dinner is in the two containers. I added a mini bottle of my homemade salad dressing you used to crave."

"But you said you wanted to cook my favorite lasagna for me."

"I did. It's in the container."

Don continued to stand in place, his mouth open without words spilling out.

"Don't tell me you thought I was cooking for us to share a meal, here, in my apartment? We haven't done that in years. Five years. But I get it. The roses, that is. And the wine. And a new sweater," she said, noticing how spiffy he looked.

"Can I at least come in and share a drink with you?"

"Might as well," she said, softening and liking the attention, smiling as she went into the kitchen to get a cork screw and another glass.

Don closed his mouth, opened and poured the wine, then took the liberty of sitting down on her couch, the one she had recovered in charcoal gray after they split. It was a color he had wanted years ago, but she felt it was too masculine and had selected a chintz floral print. Now that he no longer lived there, the place looked exactly the way he preferred.

"Martha, did you ever dream about killing me? Or think about it?"

"Why, do you think I'm going to poison you with dinner," she said, "or is this the new Don trying to woo?"

"I'm serious. Are those thoughts you had? Killing me instead of divorcing?"

"The idea might have crossed my mind, but I'd never act on it. Thinking about it and saying it out loud are obviously different. Is that what you wanted to hear?"

"I guess so. You see, I'm searching for a motive for this Jill babe, the one I think murdered Blonde Girl From The Park and Silver Fox. Nothing connects each crime except sex and maybe blackmail. I'm not sure about the blackmail because the victims died before they revealed anything and it appears that she has money. I'm wondering if her motive is the same that thousands of women have thought but don't act on."

"You talking about infidelity?"

"Yeah," he said, taking a sip of his wine.

"Yours or in general? And don't you dare spill the wine on my new couch."

"Very funny."

"Well let's tackle in general," she said. "It's bigger, yet easier. Unfaithful, cheating, breaking a promise, adultery, extramarital affair, one-night-stand, whatever you call it, the betrayal can be devastating," Martha said, challenging him with her direct eye contact.

"I know all the definitions. Remember, I went through therapy. And I know all the possible reasons.

Martha, you can't imagine how sorry I am that I hurt you. I apologized and I'll apologize again."

Martha put down her glass of wine and let out a grunt sounding laugh. "I thought we were talking in general, or about your murder suspect."

"We are, but I still love you."

"I love you, too," she said, with tears filing her eyes, then shaking her head to clear away all thoughts.

"Does that mean we can try again?"

"Trust is still an issue."

Before he could defend himself, the doorbell rang.

"Hello, Steve," she said, in a cheerful voice.

Don picked up his portable dinner, said good-bye and slipped out the door before Martha could introduce her new man. Outside, he couldn't get his feet to move, couldn't leave the area. Instead, he found a tree to lean against and waited, wondering if the guy would stay for dinner. Then he remembered the table was set for one. Don stayed, biding his time.

About 15 minutes later, Steve left, carrying a similar package, presumably with lasagna and salad. As Don wondered if Martha's new man also received salad dressing, he edged behind the tree, trying to become invisible, or at least less noticeable. The last thing he wanted was to be accused of snooping, something that came naturally to him.

Once Steve disappeared around the corner, Don went back to Martha's. He stood there, debating with himself. Should he try again or not? Would she send him away or reject him again? At last, he convinced himself to ring the bell. At the same time, Martha opened the door holding a glass of wine in one hand. She looked a little flushed from drinking.

"Hello," she said. "Why am I not surprised to see you?"

"I came to finish my drink. And help you set the table for two. I even brought dinner," he said, winking and holding up his tub of lasagna.

# Chapter 19

The murder of Blonde Girl From The Park was life-changing for Jack. All he craved was his family. Instead of being an occasional hands-on dad, he decided to cook breakfast then take his daughters to school before opening the gallery. Caroline appreciated her extra time in bed and the berry, banana, orange juice smoothie he brought to her. The girls loved the pancakes or home fried potatoes and scrambled eggs that replaced Froot Loops and milk.

Jack made a game out of cleaning up with the twins, then treasured walking the few blocks to class with one girl holding each hand, cherishing their giggles when he tried to skip the way they did.

"Daddy, tell us another knock-knock joke," Carrie said.

"Tomorrow. I need to think of one."

"Tell us two tomorrow," Carly said. "And can you get me ice cream after school like Carrie had?"

"Carrie, how did you get ice cream?"

"Our cousin gave it to me on the playground."

"What cousin? What are you talking about?"

"The nice lady who brings me ice cream. Last time, it was bubblegum flavor."

Jack stopped walking and bent down to be at eye level with his daughter. "What does this lady look like?"

"Nice, with pretty eyes and long dark hair. And she smells really good."

"Was she inside the school property?"

"She was outside of the playground behind the wire fence. She called me over to her. Just me. Not Carly. Not any of my friends. She says I'm special."

"When was this?"

"Yesterday, during afternoon recess and the day before during morning recess. And one more time before that."

"See, Daddy. It's not fair," Carly said. "Why should Carrie get ice cream and not me? I don't like this cousin."

Jack stayed down, pulling the girls close onto his bent knees, trying to figure out how to warn them of danger without frightening them.

"Remember how we talked about never speaking to strangers," he said.

"But Daddy, she's not a stranger, she's our cousin," Carrie said. "And she brings me ice cream."

"You don't have any cousins. I'll get both of you all the ice cream you want. First, you must promise never to speak to this lady again."

Carly nodded while Carrie pursed her lips and kept still.

Jack hurried the girls into school, ready to tell the head master and the kids' teacher about the menace to students' safety. His mind created scenes of parents alerted to a possible kidnapping and classes receiving safety lectures. Was this necessary if his children were the only ones targeted?

After bringing his daughters inside, he imagined police and undercover agents stationed around the building. No matter how many law enforcement people were assigned, Jack feared the cops couldn't safeguard the kids. His fear was palpable, paralyzing him.

"I have to…I have to…I have to…" he said to himself, unable to make a decision. He needed immediate advice from a pro. Jack stepped outside and dialed Don. The line was busy.

"Maybe you can tell the girls three knock-knock jokes," said a familiar voice.

Jack swung around and saw Jill behind the school fence. She was in costume, dressed like a member of the school cleaning crew with a school badge around her neck.

"What are you doing here?" he said, trying to sound normal while his eyes twitched. Her abundance of perfume tickled his nose, forcing a sneeze.

"I just want to be friends. Especially with Carrie, the one who looks like you. She's so cute, maybe I'll keep her. You have two, a spare you don't need, right?"

"Go away! For God's sake, leave us alone," Jack said, taking deep breaths, anger making him tremble. "I delivered your fucking package in London. Now, get out of my life."

"You're the only living person who knows all about me. Not to worry. I like you. That's why I told your daughter we're special pals, like cousins."

"You do know you're wanted for murder, right?"

"There's no proof."

"Does that mean you're admitting guilt?" he said, frantically redialing Don.

"Never. However, the less authorities know about me, the better it is for you and your family, especially Carrie."

"That sounds like a threat," Jack said, severing the call.

"Let's just agree there are good reasons not to tell anyone you saw me."

Jack stood helpless, avoiding her dagger-like eyes.

"See you tomorrow," she said with a big smile before sauntering off.

He tried to muster the courage to call his wife. He dialed then hung up, unable to face her fear, confident the girls were okay as long as they were in class. He also tried Don again, relieved to be connected.

"You schmuck. What the fuck are you waiting for? Get into the school and alert them ASAP," Don said. "I'm calling the police. You call Caroline and wait for me inside."

As Caroline approached the school, she saw two police cars. She raced into the building to find the headmaster and Carrie's teacher talking to Jack and her father. Jack put his arm around her.

"We're on top of it," he said.

"On top of what? What the hell's going on?"

Then she looked at Carly who was sitting on a chair next to a teacher's aide. The little girl jumped down and hugged her mother.

"Where's Carrie?"

"We think Jill borrowed her," Don said.

Caroline was about to lose control.

"Borrowed?" she said.

"For a short while," Don said.

"What do you mean? What are you saying?"

"Jill's pattern has been to buy Carrie ice cream, enjoy her company and then disappear. Sometimes she brings the ice cream. Other times Jill takes Carrie with her."

"Other times! It's happened before and nobody told me!"

"We just found out today. Carrie informed me this morning," Jack said. "Don and I discussed it and decided not to alarm you until we have more facts."

"And do you?"

"Do I what?"

"Have more facts. You're making me crazy."

"Not really. We know Jill has showed up over the past few days during morning or afternoon recess. She usually gives the ice cream to Carrie through the wire fence."

"I told her not to take it," Carly said.

"Do you know where they went to buy the ice cream?" said Caroline.

"No. I wanted to go with them, but Cousin only chose Carrie. Maybe next time it'll be my turn."

"You don't have any cousins and you are never, ever, ever to go with her or any other stranger anywhere. Do you understand?"

"I do too, have a cousin," Carly said, then burst into tears.

"How can teachers allow this?" Caroline shouted. "Isn't anyone watching the students on the playground?"

"It was crowed and noisy. They claim they didn't notice. Maybe she was captured on the surveillance cameras," Jack said.

"Jill is risking getting caught coming here and establishing a pattern," Don said. "She'll probably shake up her routine today. Go for the unexpected."

"Honey," Jack said, "it appears that Jill favors Carrie. I don't think she'll harm her because she likes her. At least that's what Jill told me."

"You talked to her?" Don and Caroline said at the same time.

"This morning, when I dropped off the kids."

Caroline mustered all her lawyer-like strength to stay erect. She dragged her husband outside. Don followed.

"Why didn't you call me immediately? While I'm doing mundane things, going to the gym, the cleaners, Carrie's in danger. I thought we're a team."

As they continued to argue, Jack got a whiff of Jill's perfume again. He turned every which way, but didn't see her. Then Carrie tugged on his leg.

"Daddy, the other day I got chocolate with cherries inside. I went to the ice cream store. I can show you where to get some for Carly."

"You are never to go with her again," Jack said.

"She told me she's going away for a little while so I won't see her."

Meanwhile, Don arranged for two plainclothes cops to be on the school grounds during class time. He also provided a photo of Jill for the school to distribute. It wasn't enough for Caroline.

"Homeschooling," she said. "Our girls are not going to class until this lunatic is found and locked up! Do you understand, Jack?"

"I understand. It's the only thing that's made sense all day."

"Cousin promised she'd find me when she comes back," said Carrie. "I'm going to get mint chocolate chip."

# Chapter 20

"Jack, it's me, Oliver."

"I know. I see your name on my phone. What's up?"

"I had to close the gallery this morning."

"Why?"

"I've been questioned by the police all day."

"Why? What for?"

"For the murder of the Blonde Girl From The Park."

"That's impossible. We were together with lots of people. You have an alibi that's as good as mine and they let me go."

"Righto, but my semen was found in the dead girl's body. The situation is bloody awful."

"Oliver, this is a joke, right?"

"If only."

"How is this possible?"

"How?"

"I understand how. I mean when did you have time? You spent the day organizing the opening event, then stayed with me and Caroline while the guests showed up."

"You know how organized I am. The party was set up way before necessary. I had lots of time."

"Did you already know this girl?"

"Sort of. Never got her name. She came by a few times the week before the opening. Threw herself at me. Quite the crumpet. Happy as could be. Why not, I thought."

"Where?"

"You want to know where we did it?"

"Not my office. Please tell me it wasn't in my office."

"I have my own office, and my own apartment, though where is not the question you should be asking. What do I do now? The girl is from the states, I think New York City, but I'm not sure. One good thing is that they found someone else's DNA under her nails."

"That helped clear me so it should clear you, unless they think you killed her with an accomplice."

"I'm sure that's one of their theories. Jack, I need all the help I can get. Maybe you can call your father-in-law."

"I'll call Don the minute we hang up. And don't worry about the gallery. From what you've told me before, people are coming by to look at the crime scene rather than the art. We'll keep it closed for a few days Anything else you can tell me about the girl?"

"She wore a wedding band. This is gonna muck up my life. The whole thing's a bit wonky and I'm knackered."

"For God's sake, speak English. And tell me everything about the victim."

"If you call Don, I'll tell both of you at the same time."

"Oliver, I only met her in the park around noon the day she was murdered. I need to hear anything you can remember."

"You picked her up! You married devil."

"No. I was delivering a package—cookies someone gave me to give to her. I really don't know her at all.

"You probably think you're making sense, but trust me, you're not."

"Tell me more about the girl. You must have learned something screwing around for almost a week. Was she afraid of anything?"

"The police asked me the same question. Nothing that I noticed. She was bubbly and available and horny. So am I, available, that is, so why not?"

"You're holding back. I can tell there's more."

"There is one thing. She said she was married. Her husband was upset she went to London without him. He didn't know she cheated and according to Blondie, he had no idea she sometimes swung both ways. Kinda turned me up a notch, which is fine since she's not my wife."

"I knew she was married."

"You put on a pretty good innocent I-don't-know-this-girl act when the body was discovered. Why would someone ask you to give the girl cookies?"

"Long story. I'll tell you some other time."

"Save it until after you call Don. I think I also need a barrister here."

"I'll phone my father-in-law now. Stay put."

"Ha ha," Oliver said. "Tell Don Blonde Girl brought the look-alike doll with her the last time we were together. She loved it. Said it was an adorable present from a friend. I asked the police for the name of the company that made it, but they won't tell. Maybe Don can find out and then see who ordered it."

"He has that info already. There was another murder in New York with another look-alike doll."

"So that means the killer is back in the states, assuming it's the same person."

"Don's convinced it's the same person. If he can assure your law enforcement that the specifics of both cases are the same, maybe they'll lose interest in you."

"Who's the killer, Jack? This is no time to be silent."

"Someone I met in the states. A crazy, dangerous woman."

"Tell the Brits, my friend, and get me off the hook."

"Don is working on it with Caroline. I'll fill them both in."

"If the murderer is so dangerous, do you really want Caroline involved? You should tell her not to participate."

"You don't know Caroline. She's her own boss. That's one of the reasons I fell in love with her. Before I get them involved, you have to tell me more about Blonde Girl. They won't care about the stuff I want to know."

"There's not much more I can add. It's not like we had a long-term relationship. She seemed carefree and troubled at the same time. Young, no kids. Had a puppy that she was crazy about. Even showed me its photo. She worked as an assistant in a financial company. I think she planned to fly home the day after our artist's reception, mentioned something about cookies as her last assignment. What's with cookies all of a sudden? You thinking of becoming a baker?"

"Forget it. I'm calling Don right now."

"Wait a minute. The time of the murder is also in question. You and I thought it was when the music got terribly loud. The police think it was earlier, which makes it closer to the time I was with her. In my office, if you really need to know. After, she went to the loo to freshen up before going to her hotel to leave the doll and change into something sexier. She wanted to get rid of anything neon. I guess she never did.

# Chapter 21

Blonde Girl From The Park had a name she hated. What mother calls her daughter Sinclair? The Internet says it's of Scottish origin and works for a girl or a guy. Most people who heard her name mentioned Sinclair Lewis. Her mother was not a writer, didn't read books and her family did not have a Scottish heritage. Sinclair couldn't understand why her mother burdened her like this. Her father never intervened, so Sinclair it was.

As a kid, she had many nicknames: Sinny which changed to Skinny because she was so thin. Claire, that morphed to Clair de Lune and then Luney, which sounded crazy. Her dad called her his wild child when she abandoned curfews and hooked up with a group of teens who smoked pot and rode motorcycles. Her friends called her stubborn because once she decided to try something, no one could stop her.

She hid her distaste for all the labels behind a wide smile and wonderful laugh, earning the reputation of a fun person.

Sinclair's husband was the first to find a solution she really liked. He called her Blonde Girl. They met in high school and married young, moving from the suburbs to lower Manhattan. He decided to go into real estate. She entered the corporate world as an administrative assistant. They rescued a puppy, a little mutt. Wanting to be a good wife, she learned how to be a sort-of cook. Life was good until she screwed it up.

Sinclair was restless. She enjoyed sex with her husband, yet wanted new experiences. Maybe having a unisex name meant she could go either way. Probably, it didn't mean anything, but she decided to experiment. The Downtown Bar and Grill was close to her apartment. She often passed it when walking her dog. One evening, while her husband was taking another real estate class, she wandered over, without her pet.

Inside, was a young crowd. Judging from their business attire, she assumed they were taking a break with a quick beer or glass of wine between work and home. She grabbed the last empty seat at the long bar and ordered a Coors, taking her time to survey the crowd. Many people seemed to be regulars, or at least were engaged in friendly conversations as if they already knew each other.

Just as she was beginning to feel out of place, an elegant woman sat next to her, flipping back her long black hair.

"What are you drinking," she said.

"Coors."

"I'll have the same."

"You can share my chair," Sinclair said, staring into the most amazing deep blue eyes.

"Thanks, but I like to stand. Been sitting all day. I'm Jill. I see you're married," she said, holding Blonde Girl's hand and fondling her wedding band. "Ever been with a woman? Some guys don't count that as cheating.

They think it's an extra perk, maybe even hope you bring home your new partner."

Blonde Girl was startled and pulled her hand away, staying, while tapping her foot that showed how nervous she was. She wondered if there was something about herself that encouraged the woman to approach her for a same sex encounter. Maybe later, she would ask. Right now, she could hardly believe her latest desire could really happen. It was so abrupt she wasn't sure she would follow through.

Jill placed her index finger in Blondie's glass, circled the girl's mouth with a trace of the cold beer, then put her finger in her own mouth. Blondie's eyes were open wider than her mouth.

"I have a conference call with an extremely nasty warlord in Hong Kong at midnight," the woman said. "Would you like to come to my place over on Eleventh Street? You have to be out by eleven forty-five. Every call is via teleconferencing these days and I'll need time to fix the total mess you're going to make of my hair and make-up."

Blonde Girl flashed her broad smile. Since she had made up her mind about what she wanted before she walked into the bar, it didn't take long for this stunning woman to convince her to go home with her.

"No problem. I have to be home way before that. My husband's class is over at nine and I promised him a late dinner."

Blondie was so nervous, she neglected to look around the apartment, didn't notice how sparse it was, with an unlived-in feeling. She didn't know how to begin, so she just stood there until Jill kissed her. On the mouth. Then took her hand to lead her into the bedroom.

It wasn't until after they were both satisfied, together on the bed, yet separate, that Jill hit her with her proposition.

"I'd like you to do a favor for me," she said, as they rested naked in bed with their legs intertwined.

"I'm going to London and wonder if you would fly over a few days earlier. I'll pay your way, of course, and your hotel bill."

"Why would you do that? I haven't taken a vacation from my job yet. I think my husband expects us to go somewhere together."

"No husband. Just you. We can have sex again, in Europe, or not."

"If not, why are you inviting me? And why must I go earlier?"

"Better not ask too many questions. I expect a package to arrive before my schedule lets me get there. I'll arrange for someone to give it to you. Take the package, hold on to it until I join you, then give it to me and go home. It's really simple."

"If it's so simple, why don't you do it?"

"The package is from someone who doesn't like me, so I need an intermediary person." It was a lie. Jill liked to play games with people and intended to be in London and watch Jack and Blondie from a distance.

"What's in the package and can't your hotel hold it for you?"

"Too many questions. Yes or no?"

"No?"

"Trick question. You won't say no," Jill said, beaming the visual of their encounter across her ceiling. "Surely you don't want your husband to see this."

Sinclair screamed, feeling trapped. She didn't want anyone to know that her wild side had escaped for a brief encounter.

"Look, if you fly to England and deliver my package," Jill said, "I'll give you this flash drive and your life can return to normal."

"That's blackmail. I can't pay you much to give me the evidence."

"I don't want your money. I have plenty of my own. All you have to do is fly to England and follow my instructions."

In London, Blonde Girl's directions were to be friendly to someone named Oliver, the manager of a posh art gallery not far from Claridge's hotel where she was staying. Oliver was cute. His light brown skin was different from anyone she had been with. She immediately decided to include him among her latest conquests. He took her to a great restaurant. She took him back to her room. They got together each of the three days before Jill arrived.

Once Jill showed up, Blonde Girl had to be clandestine. She didn't want Jill to get jealous. When a package arrived for her with a neon green jacket, and matching sneakers with hi-top shoelaces, she put them on as if she were donning a costume, feeling as if she were in a play taking on the role of a seasoned spy. Her next instructions were to go to the Reformer's Tree in Hyde Park and wait for a man in neon sneakers to approach her. Even her encounter with Jack in the park was better than she had hoped. The whole trip was turning out to be such fun.

Blonde Girl raced to the gallery to see Oliver one last time before changing for the cocktail party. Her moments with him were amazing. Maybe it was being in London. Maybe it was being illicit. Maybe it was having sex in his office.

"I really have to stop this," she said to herself before dashing to the bathroom to clean up. Jill was inside the loo, handing her a beer that had already been poured. Blondie wasn't in the mood for a drink, but did not want to anger Jill. She gulped it down hoping to get out of their as soon as possible.

The room soon began to spin and become blurry. As Blondie slipped to the floor, Jill wrapped a new pair of extra-long neon laces around the girl's neck. Blonde Girl tried to pull them off, scratching skin on Jill's hand in an attempt to save her life.

# Chapter 22

"Hey, Martha. I have a project for you," Don said, on one of his now frequent phone calls.

"I have enough projects of my own."

"Come with me. We can do it together."

"Together was long ago."

"This one will help Jack."

"What's the project?"

"Meet me over on West 36th Street. I have an appointment to see a top-notch place that makes custom dolls and puppets. Real professional. You can scope them out while I ask some questions."

"If I agree, don't get any cozy ideas."

"Me? Cool as can be. I'm after your eyes and brain. This time."

"Will you identify yourself as a detective?"

"Not sure. We'll start as a couple looking to make matching dolls for our anniversary. How many years would it be?"

"Including the years after our divorce?" said Martha.

"Of course."

"Fifty."

"Pretty nice number. Maybe we should buy a set for ourselves."

"To keep at my place or yours?"

"Very funny," said Don.

"Are you talking about Bobbleheads?" said Martha.

"No. I'm talking about the dolls I told you were found next to the two murder victims, the one in London and the one with Silver Fox in New York. They're more like ventriloquist's dummies. I found the company that made them. My goal is to find out who bought them."

"What does one of these custom things cost?"

"From what I found online the simplest version can run as high as $1,500. The more details, the greater the price."

"That's a pretty hefty investment to leave as a calling card when knocking someone off."

"Jill, our only suspect, has money, or at least spends it."

"I wonder why she doesn't strangle someone without a matching doll," Martha said.

"Maybe she's trying to be unique."

"The neon green laces would be enough."

"I agree," Don said, "except we're dealing with a nutjob. The problem is that even if we can prove Jill bought the dolls, it's not enough to convict her."

"So why bother?"

"We never know what fact will lead to another. Sometimes circumstantial evidence is enough to sway a jury, especially if we can get a sample of her DNA to match the skin under Blondie's nails.

"Don, much as I'd like to check this place out, I think you should go with Caroline. I'll stay at her apartment to watch the kids."

Don nodded into the phone, even though Martha couldn't see him.

"I knew you'd say that, but it was worth a try," he said. "My appointment's at 10:00. How about lunch after so I can fill you in on any discoveries."

Martha closed, then opened her mouth, moved her head from left to right. "Why not?" she said, happy to be included.

\*\*\*\*

Don and Caroline took a cab over to the West side in the heart of the garment district. Racks of clothes were pulled along the sidewalk by workers who unloaded trucks of coats, jeans, blouses and dresses to deliver to offices where buyers for stores could select next season's merchandise. Everyone outside seemed to be walking with a purpose.

Father and daughter entered an old building and quickly located a listing for the doll company posted in the lobby directory. The oversized elevator was slow, yet efficient, despite a few creeks. As they neared the seventh floor, they could smell paint or turpentine.

The minute they arrived they knew they were inside a very professional, artistic studio. The place took up the entire floor. Photos on the walls showed dolls that Caroline had seen on TV shows. Artists in one section were sitting on high chairs at equally high work tables, busy painting faces made of polyurethane and coated with rubber. They could hear the whir of sewing machines in another area where people were making costumes for the figures. In one corner, someone was hammering wood into miniature shoes.

High ceilings with old ornate molding made the room feel even larger. The wide-planked wooden floor was strewn with scraps of cloth and splatters of paint. Strong modern lighting made it feel as if it the room was filled with sunshine.

"Welcome," said the manager, dressed in jeans and a T-shirt. "I'll be glad to show you around, answer any questions you might have. Just don't touch anything and watch your clothes. You don't want to get paint on yourself."

"Thanks. And thanks for agreeing to see us," Don said, taking the lead. "Do many people come here to buy a doll or puppet?"

"Most order online. Since they're expensive, many buyers represent companies seeking items for a corporate event, a marketing opportunity, a film or show or advertisement. Other buyers include film producers or celebrities. I'm not at liberty to tell you their names."

"Understood. I have a confession. I'm not a potential customer. I'm a detective investigating two murders that included your dolls," Don said, taking out his badge.

"My dolls! How's that possible?" the manager said.

"Each victim had a look-alike, an exact replica of his or her face. We traced them to your company. You do a damn good job," Don said, as he showed the manager a photo of Blonde Girl From the Park and another of Silver Fox. "These look familiar?"

"Absolutely. They were ordered by the same person. The requests came through online along with a photo."

"Do you have a name?"

"John Doe."

"No shit. You took the order that way."

"The guy paid, so why not? It's just a doll. No crime in that. Same person bought one a year ago and another the year before that."

"Was a credit card used?"

"Yes, I remember it was American Express Platinum. Give me a minute and I can find the name."

While the manager went into his office, Don joined Caroline at the other end of the studio.

"Daddy, this place is freaking me out. There are boxes of fake eyeballs, hands, and legs resting on metal shelves. The workers told me they start with a sketch or photo with front and side views, then carve the head out of wood before making a mold to fill with polyurethane. They also need to sew the costume. It's a combination of engineering and craftsmanship and takes weeks to complete an order."

"Talk about premeditated. Our perp is a planner who is well organized."

Just then, the manager caught up with them.

"Brian Fisher," said the manager. "The card belongs to a Mr. Brian Fisher. The dolls were sent to PO Box 224 in Greenwich, Connecticut."

"So much for John Doe. This might be the killer's first mistake. According to Silver Fox, Fisher was Jessica's last name. Brian must be a relative, probably her father," Don said. "Could be her accomplice or maybe she's just using his credit card."

Caroline admired the detailed work of the artists until she stopped at a section of molded heads.

"Dad! Dad! Look at this," she said.

Don rushed over to find two 18-inch dolls, similar to the one Silver Fox had. The first was completed, a good-looking man the detective didn't recognize. Balanced next to it was an unfinished one. The head was fully sculpted though not yet painted.

"It's Jack," Don said. "The head looks like Jack. He's on our killer's list."

## Chapter 23

"Mommy, I have a problem. I need to talk to you," Caroline said to Martha while her mother cut slices of apple pie to go with their coffee.

"Uh oh. It must be a big problem. You haven't called me Mommy in years."

Caroline nodded, then sighed.

"You baked! I don't remember eating homemade pie or cookies growing up."

"I have more time now," Martha said. "It's good to tackle something new. Your father has been delighted to be my taster, though he likes everything so he's not much help."

"Are you two getting back together?"

"We are together, separately."

"I don't understand."

"Let's just say that after 50 years, we're in sync and leave it at that for the time being. Who's with the girls?" she said, shifting the topic.

"Jack. He's taking another turn at home schooling. He has way more patience than I have and is a much better teacher. He loves working with the kids. Mom, he can't know about our discussion today. Promise me you won't say a word to him."

It was Martha's turn to nod, then wait quietly for her daughter to share her situation.

"Mommy, this week I decided to bring Jack's favorite navy blazer to the cleaners. He came home late one night reeking of cigarette smoke. I figured the smell would air out, but it didn't."

"Is this about him coming home late?"

"Yes. I mean no. Well, that, too, but coming in at 1:00 AM and cigarettes are only part of the problem. When I pulled the jacket off its hanger, it felt heavy on one side. I checked the pockets and you won't believe what I found. It was shocking, terrifying, mysterious, horrifying."

"What could possibly be there that caused such a reaction from my strong, always-face-problems, girl?"

"A gun."

"A gun. Like the one Daddy carries."

"I guess," Caroline said, surprised at her mother's calm reaction. "Maybe it isn't so horrifying to you because you married a cop. Daddy always kept his work separate and I think I only saw his pistol twice while growing up. Both times, I walked into the den while he was cleaning it."

"You realize that after Carrie was, shall I say borrowed, and you found a look-alike doll at the manufacturer that looked like Jack, he might want to be able to protect the twins and defend himself."

"The timing is off, Mom. Jack brought the gun home before I visited the doll place with Dad and before Carrie was whisked away for ice cream by that woman.

He got the weapon just before we went to London for his event, before we discovered a dead girl at his gallery."

"It takes over six months to get a permit and license. From what you've told me, not enough time has gone by for him to have the weapon legally. How did he get it and where's the gun now?"

"I have no idea how he got it, though it must have something to do with the night he came in late. As shocked and angry I was at Jack, instead of confronting him, I hid the gun in one of my drawers. Funny how one good secret breeds another."

"Ah, secrets. They can destroy any relationship."

"Did you and Daddy have secrets?"

"I don't know of any, except his affair. That's a big enough deception to put an end to a marriage. Might explain why we're together, separately," she said.

Caroline nodded, patting her mother's hand as a gentle sign of support.

"At first, I was afraid to touch the gun," Caroline said. "I don't even know if it's loaded. I have no idea how to check."

"Ask your father. If anyone can lend a hand with this, it's Don."

"No. Absolutely not. I'm helping him for the first time, and I like it. I have no intention of becoming part of his list of problems."

"Let me get this straight. Jack has a secret from you. You have a secret from Jack and now you also have a secret from your father while you're working with him."

"Right. And I hate secrets. All I do is think about what I can and can't say. It's created a rift between Jack and me and is making me nervous."

"Did you come here for my advice or just to unburden yourself?"

"Both," Caroline said.

"Then I have a few questions. Do you want to punish Jack and the woman he may or may not have had a tryst with?"

"I would have to find out if something happened between them first."

"So, you want to eliminate the gap that secrets created between you and your husband."

"I think so," Caroline said. "I feel like you're leading me to talk to Jack, find out what happened, give him a chance to explain."

"That's exactly what I'm advising, but only you can decide whether you're ready for the truth."

"What if I don't like what he tells me?"

"That's the risk. I believe it's better than acting out of ignorance. You've never avoided facing difficulties. Maybe you can consider this a snag. Sounds less nasty, don't you think?"

"Some snag. You make it sound simple."

"I know it's not simple. Trust is a tough thing to restore. It's been five years since your father strayed. You know we've been through therapy alone and together. Possibly it helped us. Don proclaims his love, insists he's changed. Supposedly, infidelity doesn't have to be a deal-breaker, but it was so hurtful to hear what he did it still makes me wary about patching up our connection. At the same time, our bond cannot be denied."

Caroline had no words to offer so she got up and hugged her mother.

"I think our little talk is helping me more than you," her mother said, returning the hug."

"My situation is different. Jack didn't have an affair. Chances are he had a quick out-of-marriage experience, an unplanned thing with a stranger, though it's a gut feeling and I have no way of knowing for sure. I know he was curious so I told him to go do it. I kind of gave him permission for a one-time pass."

"Did you mean it?"

"I thought I did at the time. I even reminded him that what he could do, I could do, just to show him how it felt to think about me with someone else."

"Do you want to experiment? If you both do, there could be something wrong in your relationship, something that needs to be addressed and hopefully, fixed."

"I don't want to. And I don't want Jack to. I keep hoping that the night he came in late he met up with the killer, Jill, and she just sold him the gun."

"The only way to find out is to talk to your husband, your best friend since high school, the dependable father of your children, the man who likes to cook for you and brings art and joy into your life. He's successful in business and loves you so much he agrees to do everything your way. I can go on and on, but you get the gist. He's a perfect match for my pushy girl."

"Even if Jack and I get past the secrets, I'm terrorized Jill will kidnap Carrie and kill my husband."

"Like I said, talk to your father. This is his area of expertise and he knows all the facts. You don't have to tackle this by yourself. Let the professionals help you."

"Daddy and the police believe Jill is a murderer. They can't arrest her without evidence. She's slippery."

"She'll make a mistake sooner or later. They all do," her mother said, while wrapping up two packages of homemade cookies for the twins.

"As long as she's free, she's a threat."

While mother and daughter continued to talk, Caroline felt a plan of action crystalizing. Despite what Martha told her, she was not going to confront her husband or ask her father for help. Instead, she was beginning to visualize tracking down Jill then shooting her.

As a prosecuting attorney, she was confident she'd be able to figure out a way to make it look like self-defense, to be cleared and not face jail time. If she lost her right to practice law for carrying an illegal weapon, so be it. At least her children and Jack would be safe. And it might be enough revenge to avoid discussing the possible tryst with her husband.

# Chapter 24

Caroline and Don drove up to Connecticut to the Greenwich police station. The minute Don flashed his badge and identified himself as an ex-cop turned private eye, he was welcomed as if he were family.

"This is my daughter," Don said, as he introduced Caroline. "Her husband discovered a dead body in his art gallery in London. It was a young girl who was strangled and we think there might be a link between that victim and one of your residents, Brian Fisher, though we haven't figured out the connection yet."

"Brian Fisher? We knew him, big donor," the officer said. "Most of the Belle Haven residents are very supportive."

"Knew him? What happened?"

"He died two years ago. The papers carried a big story about an accident while hiking in Aspen with his daughter. He fell off a trail."

"By daughter, I assume you mean Jessica," Don said. "We know she also goes by the name Jill Foster."

"If Brian is dead, he can't be an accomplice," Caroline said. "His daughter's still using his credit card. That's fraud. We can probably pick her up on identity theft even if she was an authorized user while he was alive."

"I prefer to keep her out there until she makes a bigger mistake and we get her for murder. We don't know where she is. We have no idea where she went when she moved out of her apartment."

"Maybe she moved back to her house."

"Maybe. I think it's time to delve deeper. Let's start with the people next door."

"What's Fisher's address?" Don said to the officer.

"It's in an exclusive area where Ethel Kennedy's nephew, Michael Skakel lived," he said while writing it down. "He's the guy who was sent to jail for Martha Moxley's murder when they were both teens."

"I knew this babe had money," Don said.

"If you want to look at the Fisher house, I can drive you over in one of our cars."

"Thanks, but first I'm going to try to get a meeting with one of their neighbors."

"Hillary Halleron. That's the one you want. Her son, Eddie, married Jessica."

"We should talk to him," Don said. "Is he living in her house?"

"Eddie died. Drowned in the bathtub. Accidental death involving sleeping pills and alcohol. The house has been unoccupied ever since, though not for sale."

"Sounds shady, especially after Jessica's father had a fatal accident as well."

"Believe me, we're aware of the circumstances. We investigated Eddie's death and couldn't nail his wife. We have to assume she's innocent."

"Daddy, it feels like something is off here. I bet Brian's death was no accident."

"It sure is a strange set of coincidences," said the officer. "We spoke with the Aspen police. They couldn't come up with anything other than it was an unfortunate catastrophe. It's not the first time someone fell off that mountain. Everything was documented in their reports and written up in the newspapers."

"Come on," Don said, "we need to go to the library and read old articles."

The handsome young man behind the desk at the library took to Caroline the minute she started to ask questions.

"Where can I find reports about Brian Fisher and his daughter?" she asked.

"You mean Brian and Jessica? He was a special man, gave me an interest-free loan to continue college when my father lost his job," he said." Jessica told me to forget about repaying it after her father died."

"Rather generous," Caroline said. "I guess nobody is all bad or all good."

"She married my friend, Eddie Halleron. The poor guy died a year into their marriage. His parents live next door."

"Do you know the best way to get to the Halleron place?" said Caroline.

"Everyone does. It's part of the town gossip," he said, printing directions from his computer. I can give you his parents' home phone number in case they still use their landline."

Scheduling a meeting with Mrs. Halleron was easy considering the time lapse since Eddie's death. Maybe they would finally get some relevant information.

Driving to Belle Haven, they stopped at a small gray guard house. After guards called the Halleron's and checked Don's I.D., they drove straight up, going slowly over speed bumps, then descended a slight hill to circle the peninsula. Beautiful multi-million-dollar homes were located on perfectly manicured lots.

When Caroline rang the bell, a maid in uniform answered, brought them through a hallway that was half the size of her apartment, then escorted them into a mammoth living room with high ceilings and an abundance of ornately framed oil paintings.

Don and Caroline sat on a plush, salmon-colored couch that enabled them to face the water and look out the oversized windows to watch a few sailboats drift by. As they sipped iced tea the housekeeper had brought, a slim, blonde woman of indeterminant age floated in from one of the other rooms.

"Mrs. Halleron," Don said, getting up and extending his hand. "Thank you for seeing us so quickly. As I mentioned on the phone, I'm Detective Donaldson and this is my daughter, Caroline. We work together."

"Please call me Hillary. I'm so glad someone is finally on to Jessica. If there's anything I can do to help convict her—of anything—count me in."

"That's a lot of anger. May I ask what's caused such hostility?"

"She married my Eddie," Hillary said, then walked over to a black Steinway piano that was topped with numerous photos. "Here's a photo of them at their wedding, right here at the Belle Haven Yacht Club. The Club overlooks Captain Harbor. We were lucky it was a glorious day. That's about the only lucky part of Eddie being with Jessica."

"What do you mean?" said Caroline.

"There was a cloud over that girl. Bad things happened to people around her and she always benefitted."

"Can you give us an example?" said Don.

"Here's one that upset all of us. My son was a quiet boy, a good student, regrettably in awe of her. She knew how to be nice. At the same time, she was always in charge, telling him what to do and how to act. He told me that Jessica liked to sit next to him in school. She'd copy his answers on tests. When he needed help, she'd give him wrong replies so she got a better grade than he did. Jill even received a merit award."

"She showed her true colors early on," said Don.

"Evidently she showed them much earlier. Her mother told me that Jessica had a twin sister. Before the family moved here, when the girls were six, they were on a playground with their mom. There was an accident. I'm not sure exactly what happened, but their mother told me Jessica didn't mean to harm her sister, certainly didn't mean to end her young life."

"That's a terrible tragedy," Caroline said, hand to heart. "I feel for their mother."

"And here's another bad incident, not as tragic as a death, but one that continues to cement Jessica's deranged spirit. In high school, she was a back-up cheerleader, then became varsity when one of the top girls fell and hurt her ankle. There was a nasty speculation that Jessica had tripped her, though there was no proof."

"Perhaps it was only hearsay," Don said.

"Did the girl have at least one redeeming quality?" Caroline said.

"Rumor has it she loaned money to classmates from other neighborhoods and never expected to get it back. When you have so much, that's easy to do. I guess she was also a good daughter, yet one never knows what's really going on in someone else's home."

"Good daughter," Don said. "What does that mean?"

"She was very close to her mother. Jessica was devastated when her mom committed suicide. Something inside that girl seemed to snap, though she stayed with her father until he died."

"Looks like she forgave him," Don said.

"I doubt it. I think she remained because she didn't have a job and was too emotionally damaged to strike out on her own yet."

"With so much rage, it must have been a tough life, despite the family wealth," Caroline said.

"After her dad had that awful accident in Aspen, Eddie was ready to provide a shoulder for her to lean on. He was there almost every night. They bought guns and took shooting lessons together."

That's a strange way to grow a romance," said Don.

"She claimed she was afraid to stay alone in such a big house. I didn't believe her. She often lied to get what she wanted and she wanted to live with Eddie. He wouldn't move in unless they were married. A bit old fashioned, I know, but I was so proud of his decision. She refused to wed. After her father cheated, she said she didn't trust marriage. Hence, shooting lessons. Protection to be alone."

"But they did marry."

"They sure did. When she changed her mind, we tried to talk him out of it. Eddie claimed to be happy. I decided to believe him. What choice does a mother have? Since they still lived next door, I got to see my son when she was out."

"Eddie's death must have been tragic for you," Caroline said.

"I have this gnawing feeling that Jessica had something to do with it. First, her sister, then her mother followed by her father and my son. All people in her orbit who had something harmful happen to them."

"Why do you think she wanted to eliminate him?" said Don.

"Eddie told me there was a woman he met through work. A cute young blonde flirt who came onto him rather aggressively. He wanted to stop her without insulting her, since she was a coworker. If something happened, it wasn't a detail he would share with his mother. I think Jessica found out about the overtures and assumed the worst."

"Do you know this girl's name? We should talk to her."

"Eddie didn't tell me. He always referred to her as Blonde Girl."

# Chapter 25

"Were meatballs once alive?" Carrie said, looking at the meal her father had prepared.

"What were they?" Carly said, putting down her fork.

It was Jack's turn to take care of the girls, his usual one night a week including dinner. Caroline was free to meet her friends, dash up to Bloomingdale's, or take in a lecture at the 92$^{nd}$ Street Y. Usually, she scooted out as soon as he came back from work, especially since they were home schooling since Jill had taken Carrie for ice cream. Tonight, Caroline was lingering, checking the time on her Fitbit every few minutes. Jack didn't understand why his wife was still hanging around the apartment.

"Jack, I'm scared. Really scared," she said, in a whisper so the girls wouldn't hear her. "Jill was able to walk away with Carrie for a while. She can do it again. Then there's the doll she ordered, the one that looks like you. It means you're on her kill list."

"Don't worry," Jack said, encircling his wife with his arms, snuggling into her neck. "Don and the police will grab her before she gets to me."

"I love your optimism," she said, smiling. I know I can be a cynic, but positive thoughts are not enough this time."

"Your fears are real, honey. I've got them, too. We have to deal with them," he said, hiding the fact that his breath was rapid and his heart seemed to be pumping faster. He hoped he wasn't about to have a panic attack.

"And how do you intend to face this situation?"

"I checked the Internet and read we should be eating bananas and dark chocolate and drinking green tea. That should help calm our nerves."

"Don't be ridiculous. I'm not going to sit around drinking hot beverages while a lunatic is out there targeting our kids. And don't try to suggest a tranquilizer. I need to be alert at all times."

Caroline decided she would also check the Internet, not to stay calm, but for ways to protect their girls. After the incident at school, as far as she was concerned, the only safety net was to get rid of Jill. Permanently. She was never one to let others solve her problems. This would be no exception. Forget depression, anxiety and fear of danger. It was time to take action. At least that was her decision after her discussion with her mom.

Jack cleared the table and opened a box of organic mac and cheese. So much for real cooking. Maybe he'd bring in McDonald's next time. Kids couldn't survive only on fries and ice cream. He'd have to try quinoa. While he loved preparing meals for his family, a simple dinner was getting complicated.

Unbeknownst to her husband, this evening Caroline had an appointment for her first private lesson to shoot a rifle at a shooting range on the West side. She would have preferred to master a pistol. Though she had taken the gun that was in Jack's blazer, she didn't have a permit or license and she didn't have time to get vetted. Knowing nothing about weapons, she believed it couldn't be difficult to transfer the skill of shooting a rifle to fire the handgun she planned to conceal inside her purse. With proper lessons, and making friends with someone at the shooting range, she was sure she would learn whatever she needed to know.

Her first visit had been a mandatory safety course in a classroom. Luckily, she didn't know any of the other participants. She took notes, though some of the advice sounded like common sense: No alcoholic beverages before or during a shoot, no running or jumping or climbing with a loaded firearm, and dress correctly. Must be for people taking the rifles outside to hunt.

This evening, at the shooting range, after checking in and reviewing safety rules, Caroline put on ear plugs and special ear muffs at the same time, hoping to dull the sound. Her wraparound goggles were clear rather than colored ones preferred in the woods.

As required, she stood behind a shield and placed her right foot about 45 degrees behind her left. She put her left hand on the fore stock with her elbow down. With her right hand, she moved the butt of the gun into the hollow of her shoulder. She was so nervous, instead of shooting, she took time to breathe slowly, then aimed down the firing line at the target that seemed very far away.

"Keep your finger outside the trigger guard until you're ready to shoot," the instructor said. "Concentrate, and don't fire until I say commence firing."

Caroline wondered how close she would be when she pulled the trigger on Jill. Shooting her in the back probably would be easier than face to face. She shook her head, pushing herself to focus on her immediate task.

The first shot was a surprise. The kick to her body was greater than anticipated. Maybe her shoulder would ache the next day. Still, she thought it went well. After checking her hits, she saw her shots were way off center. Shooting was harder than she thought it would be.

When her session was over, Caroline washed her hands to rinse off any lead residue. She felt powerful. The next moment she was overcome by anxiety followed by uncertainty, wishing she could try out the pistol.

Thanks to Don and his contacts on the police force, she and Jack were able to track Jill's whereabouts via her phone. If that woman ever wanted to kidnap Carrie again, they would know when she was approaching. They could alert the police and feel as if they had some control over the safety of their family. The phone would also enable Caroline to find the beautiful lunatic when Jill was ready to kill again.

Back at their apartment, once the girls were asleep, Jack decided to check on the gun he had stolen. He had been afraid to do so all the nights his wife was home, so this was his perfect chance.

Not only could he not find the gun, he couldn't find the blazer. Caroline must have taken it to the cleaners. His breathing became intense. He hoped he wouldn't black out. He needed to think clearly and figure out what to do before his wife returned.

The weapon was dragging down the jacket on one side, so for sure, she must have removed it. She didn't mention the gun, certainly didn't question him. His secret, having a pistol, was now her secret, hiding the gun.

Why didn't she confront him? Jack would have to initiate the difficult discussion he was trying to avoid. It was imperative that he find the illegal weapon and toss it into the Hudson River.

# Chapter 26

It was good that Bill Turner liked his silver hair since he had turned gray before he turned forty. He also liked his life that included an oversized colonial house, a hefty bank account, a Porsche 911 convertible and best of all, a wife who gave up her modeling career to become a stay-at-home mom, happy to care for their two teenaged sons, organize meals and walk their two Golden Retrievers.

As a financial advisor to most of his neighbors in Greenwich, CT, he was both successful and well-respected in the community. One of his favorite clients, and yes, he had favorites, was Brian Fisher, over in Belle Haven. They golfed together, sailed together, even shared an occasional dinner after Fisher's wife committed suicide.

Sometimes, when he was at Fisher's house, Jessica was also around. She was prettier than most and liked to flaunt her good looks. As far as he was concerned, Brian's daughter dressed too sexily, almost always in black outfits that clung to her perfect body. Not the more typical Greenwich preppy look.

She would study him with her unnerving aquamarine eyes. Whenever he returned her lingering stares, she retreated, making him feel as if he had initiated a dirty-old-man overture. He smiled thinking about the game they played, and how much he relished it. Though he often went out with other women, he never dabbled with one so young or close to home. He knew this girl should be off limits.

Jessica mentioned, ever so casually, that she enjoyed getting a drink at the Downtown Bar and Grill. Turner wasn't sure if that was an invitation or idle chatter. At work, above Grand Central Station, he found himself thinking about going downtown before taking the train home. Just one drink. If she wasn't there, that would be fine. He only wanted to see what kind of environment attracted this elegant tease.

The moment he walked into the pub, he spotted her sitting on a stool at the bar. She waved him over.

"So, the great Bill Turner is slumming in my neighborhood," she said. "Perfect timing. I was just about to order a drink. What are we having?"

Her wanting to order the same drink, coupled with her welcoming demeanor, felt as if they already had an intimate friendship. He tried to warn himself to be careful, to step back. Then there were those eyes. And her hand on his leg. And the vodka gimlets. She placed her index finger into his drink, rubbed the liquid around his lips, then put her finger into her own mouth. It was time for him to leave. But he didn't.

"Bill, I have a conference call with an extremely nasty warlord in Hong Kong at midnight. Would you like to come back to my place over on Eleventh Street? You have to be out by eleven forty-five. Every call is via teleconferencing these days and I'll need time to fix the total mess you're going to make of my hair and make-up."

Bill smiled, cleared his throat, hoping he understood her intentions correctly.

"I didn't know you worked. Might be time for you to start your own financial portfolio in addition to the one your parents left" he said, cursing himself for sounding so straight. "What kind of business are you in?"

"Import/export. Are you coming with me?"

"I don't know. My wife expects me home way before your conference call. How about I come see your apartment, maybe have another drink, then be on my way."

"I'm putting this on my tab," she said, slipping off the stool. "You can pay next time, for dinner."

"Bill sat on the couch in Jessica's living room, surprised at how neat it was. Then he realized it was practically empty. No photos. No books. Some generic paintings. Nothing he expected from a girl who grew up going to the best schools, with the finest cultural opportunities, the daughter who had inherited a fortune from of a wealthy client. Something felt off.

One drink led to another and then another. He texted his wife that he would be home late, then followed Jessica into her bedroom, feeling shy about the extra pounds he had let slip on over the past ten years. As with the other liaison, Jessica filmed their encounter. This time she decided not to show it to him until after she moved her stock portfolio.

He stayed way longer than planned. After dressing, he was about to walk out the door when he overheard part of Jessica's conference call. Above some static, and voices that sounded oddly similar, he could hear bits of the conversation.

*"Chong Lai from Macao. Nothing arrived."*

*"Jill Foster from the USA. That's because we didn't send anything. There are issues."*

*"Ming Cheung from Hong Kong. To be clear, we have issues."*

While the speakers never mentioned anything specific, Bill didn't like what he heard. Despite his frequent infidelity, he had principles, especially concerning his country. Anything illegal was out of his domain. He had no idea how to poke around to see if she had clandestine business. He decided to find someone to investigate Jessica.

After hiring Don Donaldson, Silver Fox stopped thinking about his latest fling. He believed in delegating and not interfering. Everything would surface in due time. Then he received a gift, a most unusual, delightful gift, a doll that looked exactly like him. Since it came from Jessica, he found himself thinking about her again. The typed note that came with the doll said:

*You shouldn't have hired a detective. And his daughter. Naughty boy. You need to be punished. Meet me at The Downtown Bar and Grill early Wednesday night. Sit in the last booth in back. Bring along this doll.*

Bill was aroused by the note, imagining another hot night in Jessica's place. He pictured her in black lingerie though he wouldn't allow himself to envision anything painfully erotic. After all, he was a family man with morals.

Once seated, he propped up the look-alike doll opposite him, aware that other diners were staring at them. They had an eyeful when he ordered two drinks, placing one in front of the doll. Silver Fox straightened his hair, then on a whim, straightened the doll's matching hair. He took a sip of his vodka gimlet, then lifted the second drink to the doll's mouth. It really was fun.

He checked his watch, wondering when Jessica would appear and what she would be wearing. After downing the rest of his cocktail, the room suddenly blurred. His head was spinning. He leaned back against the leather seating, trying to shake off whatever was hitting him.

Soon he felt something around his neck. He wanted to pull it off, but his arms felt paralyzed. His last thought was that the doll winked at him. Of course, that was impossible.

# Chapter 27

"Hey, Martha, I have two guest passes and want to share one with you," Don said over the phone.

"Guest passes for what?"

"The gym. Caroline noticed I haven't been working out since I left the police force. She thinks I'm getting soft so she gave me two free private sessions."

"Doesn't she realize we all get soft as we get older? I guess she still has you on a pedestal."

"So, when should we sign up? We'll need appointments for the lessons."

"I hate the gym."

"How can you hate the gym? You never went to one. And you better not let the school where you teach nutrition and health know about this."

Martha smiled, enjoying the fact that Don knew her so well. "Okay. One time. Private. I'll try it. Give me a few days to buy new sneakers and gym clothes, whatever that means. Late afternoon would be best."

The next day, Martha, in a ponytail and black leggings under a loose, oversized tee-shirt, joined Don at the gym. She had stuffed a brochure on *How to Cultivate a Winning Gym Attitude* inside her bag along with her own towel, convinced the ones provided would not be sanitary or soft, though she had no intention of showering there. Don insisted on taking her photo with him in front of the entrance, something to prove to their daughter that they were trying to get in better shape.

After registering at the front desk with a cheery girl named Bambi, they filled out forms, walked down a flight of stairs to the locker rooms where they could leave their things, then met back upstairs.

"It smells in here," Martha said, blinking under the LED lights and looking around at the vast number of machines.

"Keep an open mind," Don said.

"I think I'll start with the treadmill. That's just walking. I can walk," she said, noticing emaciated young women wearing ear phones and running at a faster pace than she could ever imagine matching.

"Not while we have a private instructor. You can walk or bike on your own later, or next time."

"Next time! Not so fast."

Their instructor then came over to introduce himself. What he lacked in height next to Don, he made up for with bulk. The muscles on his shoulders reached his neck. His bulging arms popped out of his sleeveless shirt. No matter how softly he spoke or how much he smiled, one knew not to mess with this man. Whatever he told them to do, they would do.

"I, uh, want to tone up," Don said, in a less confident tone than usual, "but not quite as much as you."

"Not to worry," the guy said, laughing as he grabbed a pair of three-pound weights for Martha and ten pounders for Don. "Let's work the arms first, then add

157

the chest, back, legs and abs. Do ten reps, pause, then ten again, three times."

Don and Martha faced each other, picked up their weights at the exact same time, then started their regime, giggling like children.

You might prefer to face the mirrored wall," the trainer said, while adjusting Martha's posture, changing her weights to five pounders, and slowing down Don's pace.

As they lifted and counted to ten, they could hear men grunting at the back of the room. Some made sounds when they lifted, others when they put down massive dumbbells that clinked above the sound of music coming from an adjoining room filled primarily with women in an aerobics class.

"Oh my God," Martha said, moving behind Don so her reflection was no longer in the mirror.

"Hey, ladybug, what's going on?" the instructor said, playfully. "You trying to hide from someone?"

"No, of course not. I mean yes. Well, maybe," she said, in between counting to ten.

"Isn't that the guy you gave lasagna to?" Don said, eyeing the man's muscles.

Martha moved her head to see Mr. Andrews pumping away with great concentration. Thanks to all the mirrors, there was no way to escape being seen.

"I told him I don't do the gym," she said to Don. "What'll I say? I don't want to make him feel bad."

"Why do you care?"

"Because I'm a nice person, dummy. He seems so lonely and insecure."

"I'm lonely and insecure. Why don't you worry about me?"

"I do. You just don't know it," she said, going back to lifting her weights while moving behind her ex-husband.

After warming up, their instructor brought them to the upper level to a dozen machines. It took another 40 minutes to complete their first lesson. Martha was anxious to leave, but Steve had already joined them.

"Mr. Andrews," Martha said.

"Steve."

"Steve!" she said. "What a surprise to see you here."

"I'm here every day. You're the new one," he said, then extended his hand to Don. "I'm Steve. Welcome to my world."

Both men looked at each without smiles.

"My ex," Martha said, pointing at Don. "My co instructor when I lecture on nutrition," she said, pointing to Steve.

"Can I buy you both a drink?" Steve said, taking the lead. "There's a café downstairs."

Don was happy to follow.

"Too bad they don't serve beer here" Don said, hoping for a nice cold Heineken.

When they got to the café, Steve ordered a carrot juice made with apples and celery for Martha. Both men watched her take a cautious sip. "It's good," she said, drinking more. "Better than I expected."

Steve then handed Don a dark green mixture. Don smelled it first, then grimaced.

"It's called a Healthy Green Bomb," Steve said. "Lots of kale, spinach, avocado and celery. I think they put in a dash of vanilla, but I'm not sure."

"Looks revolting," Don said, wanting to spill it into a nearby plant.

"It's high in antioxidants, reduces bad cholesterol," Steve said.

"So does beer," Don said.

"Martha told me you can be tough, so I'm sure you'll get used to it," Steve said, raising his glass.

Don took a sip and tried not to spit. "You left out that it tastes like lawn clippings."

"And it might give you gas," Steve said, with a laugh, watching Don leave it on the counter.

As they left the gym, Don asked Martha if she had anything good in her purse. She dug into her bag and pulled out a Hershey milk chocolate bar with almonds, broke it in half and shared it with him.

"That's why I love you," he said, taking a huge bite.

They walked silently for a block, enjoying the taste of sugar.

"Tough?" Don said.

"Huh?"

"What did you mean back there? Bad tough, like hard to please or good tough like strong and protective?"

"Oh, honey, it was just a word I used on lasagna night to shut Steve up and make him leave."

"I watched him go," Don said, opening the door to a nearby pub. "Time for a tough man's real drink, ladybug. Care to join me?"

Martha smiled for the first time that afternoon.

"That's why I love you," she said, following him into the bar.

# Chapter 28

"I met Jill through my gallery manager," Jack said, leaning against the bar at the Downtown Bar and Grill. "We came here for a drink to discuss the upcoming art show without any business distractions."

"Call him. Right now. Make him come here," Don said. "I can't believe we didn't talk to him earlier."

"I doubt Jonathan can add much. As far as I could tell, at the time he didn't know her well, though he knew about her."

"At the time? What the fuck are you talking about?"

"The night I met Jill. The night she filmed us having sex and recorded it on that flash drive you refuse to give me. The night I stole her gun I can't find. Does that explain the time clearly enough for you?"

Jack startled himself, glad to be fighting back with his father-in-law even in a mild way. It felt damn good. Maybe agreeing to meet him for a drink wasn't a bad idea.

"That's the night I saw you," Don said, refusing to back down. "Start at the top. If I understand correctly, about three weeks or so ago, after closing your gallery around 5:00, you and Jonathan came downtown to my favorite bar."

Jack saw the cop side of Don, watched him take notes. It felt like he was being interrogated at a police station and he didn't like it.

"Jonathan selected the place," he said. "I know you come here. I usually stay away."

"Got it. Then what?"

"Jonathan and I tied up details for the art opening. It took less than half an hour."

"You came all the way down here for a twenty-minute conversation you could have had inside your gallery."

"I know it was crazy. If only we had stayed in mid-town, there would be no problems now."

"If. Always an if," Don said.

While Jack called Jonathan, Don picked up their drinks and carried them to a quiet booth in the back, not far from where Silver Fox had been discovered. Don was glad the place had reopened and most diners seemed oblivious to the murder that had transpired though some regulars might be intrigued to be eating at what had been the scene of a crime.

While they waited, Don tried to be nice to Jack, struggling to compliment him on his successful business and devotion to his family. It was a challenge. When he saw Jonathan, he jumped up, welcomed him, changed the subject.

"I need to ask you a few questions," Don said, flipping a page in his notebook. "Nothing official, so don't worry. Just trying to get a better handle on this Jill character, hoping to fill in some gaps, maybe even get lucky enough to find evidence for an arrest."

"Glad to help," Jonathan said, sitting down and ordering a beer.

"Tell me about her," Don said.

"Little to tell," Jonathan said, looking at Jack for some sign of how to proceed.

"You know her? Had sex with her?"

"You skip right to the heart of a situation."

"Well?"

"Yes, and no. Yes, I know her, sort of and no, I never had sex with her. She only goes with married men. She's so hot I once thought about putting on a ring and pretending I was hitched just to go home together."

"How do you know she only goes with married men?"

"She told me. Is that direct enough for you?"

Don slammed the table, annoyed at Jonathan's attitude.

"Look, we have a murderer on our hands. I'm pretty sure she killed the blonde girl at Jack's Gallery in London. Her husband keeps calling my buddy Smith, asking if the American police can do anything in the UK. I'm also sure Jill executed my client, Silver Fox. His wife and kids are devastated. Rumor has it in Connecticut that both Jill's father and husband died in her company under questionable circumstances, though nothing was ever proved against her."

Jonathan took a gulp of his beer, looked at Jack again, then nodded.

"Okay. I get it. I'm on board."

"There's more you should be aware of. Jill has a strange calling card," Don said. "She leaves a look-alike doll next to each victim. The doll manufacturer has two more she ordered. One is for a man we haven't identified and one resembles Jack. That said, is there anything else you can share that might help us get Jill behind bars before she knocks off your boss?"

Jonathan fidgeted with his beer then looked at Jack again.

"Tell me anything and everything," Don said. "Let me decide if it's useful."

"I helped her buy a motorcycle. She didn't care about the price."

"So you are friends. You never let on how well you know her," Jack said.

"Jill doesn't have friends. She uses people, then tosses them."

"That's what I thought," Don said. "Caroline and I have researched her. What we can't figure out is the motive. It's always the motive that'll shed light on the killer. I'm convinced it has to do with all her victims being married."

"I've seen her at the bar. She's always the initiator, no question about that. I've watched her look at the left hand of her prey, only having drinks with spouses."

"We know what she does. That still doesn't explain why."

"Well, she did let me buy her a drink on more than one night, when it was quiet and she wasn't hunting. It was like she allowed herself special permission to talk to me. I kind of enjoyed her. She can be charming when she wants. Now that I think about it, she never revealed much, let me do most of the speaking."

"What did you tell her?"

"I talked about being single, sometimes liking it, sometimes not. I mentioned my boss, Jack, and how he was an inspiration as a devoted family man. Even told her about his art gallery on 57$^{th}$ Street and the others in London, Paris and Florence."

"Didn't this bore her, you talking about someone else?"

"At first, I think she listened because I'm so involved with my work, or maybe because it was a quiet night. Then she asked questions about Jack, intrigued that I thought he was such a family guy. We joked about whether or not she could seduce him. Almost made a bet. It was silly. Whoever won would get a box of chocolate chip cookies. She has a thing for chocolate chip cookies, trying to find some that taste like the ones her mother made without a written recipe."

"You fucker. You set me up," Jack said.

"I only brought you there so Jill could see who you are. If you did anything with her, you did it on your own," Jonathan said.

"I ought to fire you right now."

"Take it easy. At least wait to revisit this until after the art opening."

Jack pursed his lips in an attempt to remain silent in front of his father-in-law.

"Sounds like a stupid college prank at an Ivy League school. Even stupider since you created a problem for your boss," Don said. "You two can settle this later. Right now, I need more information."

"One evening, when Jill must have been lonely, she told me she felt sad," Jonathan said. "She wished her mother were alive to go home to."

"We know her mother died. Committed suicide."

"Did you know it happened after her mom learned about her father's affair?"

"Bingo!" Don said, slapping his forehead. "I think we've got it. Can't believe it took me so long."

"What?" Jack and Jonathan said, almost in tandem.

"She's judge, jury and executioner, punishing those who go astray like her father. She probably pushed him off the trail in Colorado. If she believed Ed screwed Blonde Girl, like her mother-in-law implied, then his drowning was no accident."

Don took a big drink of his beer, remembering his own affair, grateful that Caroline wasn't crazy and Martha was still kind to him, maybe even ready to forgive.

"See guys, this meeting was a big help. Now we need evidence before Jill strikes again. Jonathan, you have to come here more often. She realizes we're on to her so she might lay low for a while, but it would be good to know if she shows up. We need to find evidence to arrest her before she strangles our mystery man and then Jack.

# Chapter 29

Jonathan wanted to keep his job, and of course, keep his boss alive so despite his discomfort, he decided to reach out to Jill and renew their fake friendship. Don was tracking her via iphone and gave him the address of her new apartment. It turned out to be just a few blocks west of the pub they used to frequent.

After work, Jonathan rode his motorcycle to her neighborhood and walked the area, disappointed he never bumped into her, forcing him to become more aggressive in his investigation. He much preferred searching for budding artists. He decided the best solution was to camp out at the entrance to her building.

The evening Jill saw him, she didn't seem surprised. Jonathan thought it odd, feeling as if she were a step ahead of him.

"Leave me alone," she said. "You're still working for Jack and probably talking to his father-in-law. You're on the other side."

"I just want to be your friend."

"That makes you a party of one."

"One is better than none," he said, with a smile.

"I don't trust you. I don't trust anyone."

While she searched her bag for her keys, Jonathan stood silently, hands in his pockets.

"Come on," he said. "Let me buy you a drink. Like old times."

"Old times? I've known you for about a month. Did Jack send you? Or Don?"

"Don," he said, lowering his head and mumbling, "though I'm not sure what I'm supposed to find out."

"They think I'm a murderer. Probably are naïve enough to assume I'll confess in a moment of sexual ecstasy."

"Well?" Jonathan said, perking up.

"Won't happen."

"The confession or the sex?"

"Both. Now that we have the ground rules clarified, you can come up for that drink."

Jonathan was surprised at Jill's shift in friendliness making him feel even more uncomfortable. Since he had never been to her other apartment, he didn't appreciate the difference between her old and new abodes and that she had moved up, economically. When he walked in, the living room was to the left, but she started her tour with the two bedrooms. One was traditional with Frette bed linen he recognized from his last girlfriend's bedroom. The other was set up as an office with filing cabinets, bookcases filled with classics as well as a large desk and a Herman Miller Embody ergonomic chair. Over the desk was a Marilyn Monroe Warhol piece.

"This has attitude," he said. "So much more interesting than his popular soup cans."

Jill ignored his comment as if she didn't care what he thought. It wasn't until they moved into the living room that Jonathan began to appreciate what a gold mine she must be worth. There was a sumptuous white couch, traditional mahogany side tables and designer lamps contrasted with a modern black and gold coffee table he had seen in a catalog.

"Expensive taste," he said.

"I like the best. Always have."

"You never mentioned what you do for a living to pay for all this."

"Didn't I tell you my parents left me a house in Connecticut? I decided to bring some of my favorite things here instead of renting another furnished place."

"You never dropped the slightest clue about your life or your past."

"I told you we aren't friends. And in case you're wondering, we never will be. I prefer to be my only confidant. It's a safer way to live."

Jonathan shifted focus.

Then he spotted a painting by Jean-Michel Basquiat centered over the couch in the living room. It would have been the first thing he saw if he hadn't been concentrating on the impact of the total environment.

"OMG," he said. "That's one valuable piece of art. Are you secretly a call girl?"

"Why is it that men always think an independent woman must be a whore, or have a sugar daddy?"

"Well, do you?"

"Actually, I have a real daddy, or like I told you, I had one. The wealth is part of my inheritance. I earned it being a good girl and by the way, Mr. Art Expert, my father bought that on eBay for just $68,000. He was rather proud of himself."

"Are you sure it's not a print?"

As she looked at him, her eyes seemed to turn evil.

"I was just testing you," he said.

"Fuck off," she hissed.

Jonathan was completely overwhelmed and wanted to leave. The most he could do for Don on this visit would be to find something with a sample of Jill's DNA, take it out of there as soon as possible and never come back. He moved closer, trying to put his arms around her, planning to pluck a hair from her head or grab a wisp off her blouse.

"What are you doing?" she said, pushing him away. "I told you, no sex."

"Okay. Okay. How about the drink you promised?"

"I have beer and water. Haven't stocked up my bar yet."

Jonathan wanted to keep a clear head and preferred water, but felt he'd look silly.

"Beer is fine. What kind do you have?"

"Guinness and Stella Artois."

"Stella," he said, hoping they would skip glasses, then after taking a slug or two, he would switch the bottles and take hers with him.

No such luck. She returned with one beer for him and a crystal glass of ice water for herself. After a few sips, he went to her bathroom where he found a hairbrush, filled with her hair. He took a few strands and put them into his jeans pocket, forcing himself to stay calm. If he did anything out of the ordinary, he worried Jill would be on to him. The last thing he wanted was to receive one of those look-alike dolls Don was talking about.

"Gotta go," he said. "My motorcycle is downstairs in a questionable spot. I don't want a ticket. Next time I'll ante up and put it in a garage."

"Let me know in advance if there is a next time. My car is in a garage. I'll have them put your bill on my account."

"What happened to your Harley?"

"I still have it. I also have my father's Porsche in the city and my mother's Range Rover up in Connecticut. And I didn't have to screw anyone to get them."

"I wish I could afford a Porsche. That's my dream car."

"So save up."

"Are you kidding? I have a year's salary of credit card debt. Unless I get a raise, a big one, I'll be paying off the balance for a very long time."

"That's plain stupid." she said. "I can make you a quick loan, interest free, like my father used to do for many people. Sometimes he did good things as well as bad."

Jonathan was startled. How could someone so evil be so nice, so generous? There had to be a catch. Maybe she was trying to buy him over to her side. That would be impossible, yet the money was so tempting.

"Pay me back when you can," she said, going to her desk and returning with her checkbook.

"So, we are friends," he said, putting his hands back into his pockets in an effort to refuse the money.

"I'm not sure I know what a real friend is," she said. "How much do you need?"

While Jonathan silently debated with himself about accepting her offer, Jill wrote out a check, tucked it into his jacket pocket, turned him around and pushed him to the door.

Outside, Jonathan looked at the check. It was more than a year's salary. He left wondering what it would be like to have enough money to buy expensive grown-up toys and not have to put up with a boss or a cranky customer. He threw away Jill's hair since sharing the sample of this girl's DNA was no longer something he intended to do. Don's request was harder than he thought. He hoped his job did not depend upon it.

# Chapter 30

"Honey, do you realize this is the first time in five years that you asked me to join you for a social moment?" Don said, eating his half vanilla and half mint chocolate chip ice cream cone. "Usually, I'm the one doing the inviting,"

Martha and Don were sitting on a bench on the High Line near the Gansevoort entrance, faces turned toward the Hudson River sparkling in front of them. A passerby might think they were an aging couple, still in love, enjoying an afternoon break.

"I hate to disappoint you," she said, relishing the sun on her face while she nibbled at her double scoop of chocolate black cherry. "This meeting is not strictly social. I'm worried about the kids."

"You mean the twins?"

"No, Caroline and Jack. Actually, Jack. Caroline is happy as long as she gets her way. Jack is happy if Caroline is content, so he gives in to all her demands. Has since high school. If we're lucky, he always will."

"It works for them, so what do you want me to do?"

"I think Jack needs some emotional support. You have to ease up on him. Be more of a friend, less of a critic."

"I can't help it. I favor my daughter. Let him get support from his parents."

"Since Nancy and Patrick moved to West Palm Beach, they're less involved. He can use a kind word," Martha said.

"They're coming up from Florida in a few days to attend the new artist's event. Jack can get lots of emotional boosts."

"And after they leave?"

Jack cheated on our daughter," Don said.

"So you've said. But how do you know for sure?"

"Jill filmed their encounter. I have the flash drive," he said, pulling it out of his pants pocket. "It was under the bed in her vacant apartment. I carry it with me, though I'm not sure why."

"She filmed them! She's crazy."

"Crazy enough to blackmail him. As far as I know, she hasn't asked for anything, yet. Jill's a wild one. Until she makes her next move, we have no idea what she wants."

"Give the flash drive to Jack," Martha said. "Let him decide how to handle his marriage."

Don moved his head from side to side, noncommittal, stuffing the evidence back into his pocket.

"Maybe this is Jill's way to make sure Jack won't testify against her in the future," Martha said.

"She also filmed the Blonde girl and my client. Two separate additional sexual encounters. Both playmates died without leaving information about any demands from their killer. I have those flash drives as well."

"Quite a collection. You could be a blackmailer."

"Ha ha," Don said, blowing out air.

"If Caroline finds out, it might destroy their relationship."

"Our daughter is tough," Don said.

"Good tough or bad tough?"

"Both. My cheating ended our marriage. If Caroline sees what her husband did, it would be worse than just hearing about it, not that knowing would be easy," Don said.

"I don't believe Jack will show the flash drive to Caroline. That would be insane. Let him have the peace of mind that he has some control over his future, no matter how fragile."

"Am I to infer that you believe our daughter should forgive Jack while you won't forgive me."

"You didn't just cheat. You had an affair. For a long time. You had feelings for someone else."

Don looked down, hoping his knees could give him a plausible response. None appeared. Martha jumped in, changing the subject.

"It's awfully nice sitting here," she said. "With you. Almost like old times."

"I miss the old times. Even the fights."

"We never fought."

"You think so?" he said, smiling. "What about my not hanging up my clothes? Or putting the cap back on the toothpaste, or the time you tripped on my shoes I left in the living room. You had a sprained ankle for a few days and refused to talk to me until it healed. Finally, I was able to get a word in."

Martha hit him gently on the shoulder. "Those weren't fights. That was marriage. The part nobody mentions. I've orchestrated my fair share of blips for you to complain about, always figuring out a deal to get what I want or simply insisting I'm right."

"You mean like calling my clothes 'outfits' and accusing me of being color blind before making me change whenever we went out. Or the week you decided to quit the kitchen and let me cook. I think I deserve some kudos for finding damn good take-out. And I've been a good dad."

"Yes, you pitched in," she said, pausing, "once Caroline was out of diapers."

By now they had finished their ice cream, including the cones. Martha put her head on Don's shoulder. It was all he needed to place his arm around her.

"Do you think we can get back together?" he said.

"We are together, separately."

"I don't want to be separately. I want it all. The good times and the fights."

"How do I know you won't cheat again?"

"You have my word, beautiful ladybug. Speaking of ladybug, what about you and that guy at the gym? Steve."

"Mr. Pumped. We never dated. Never went out. Nada. I do like that he flirts with me. Makes me feel pretty again, sexy, rather than familiar. On the other hand, he probably would take over my kitchen with all his healthy food," she said.

"Disgusting," they said simultaneously, then shared a high-five.

"Speaking of food, what's in your purse?"

"We just ate ice cream. Isn't that enough of a sugar high for one day?"

"Are you going to put me on a diet? If so, I might retract my interest in together time."

"No diets," she said, digging into her purse and pulling out an old receipt, a brush, a wallet, keys, spare glasses, lipstick, an iphone, hand sanitizer and a Kindle and placing them on the bench. "Here we go," she said, finding a bag of mixed nuts.

"I'll share them IF you promise to be nicer to Jack. Deal?

"Deal," he said, opening his palm to accept some nuts."

# Chapter 31

"If I seem a little jumpy," Jack said, when he picked up his parents at LaGuardia Airport," it's because there's so much going on."

He didn't want to scare his folks, yet they needed to know what was happening, especially if his mom babysat.

"Not just the art event. I'm talking about a murderer who specializes in killing cheating spouses, but might be after Carrie."

"Oh no," Nancy said, turning to look at her husband who was in the back seat with a huge bag of Florida oranges. "Does this have anything to do with the killer in London?"

"I'm afraid so, or at least we think it does. There was a second murder here in Don's favorite restaurant."

"There are murders all the time," Nancy said. "Why does Don think this one is connected to the disaster in your London gallery?"

"She used the same method. Drugged her victim then strangled him with extra-long neon shoelaces and left a look-alike doll."

"She?" You know who it is?"

"Don thinks the killer's a woman named Jill. A beautiful lunatic, according to Jonathan, who knows her from the bar scene."

"What's a look-alike doll?" Patrick said, ignoring the implication that his son spent time at bars.

"Exactly what it sounds like. A doll with the same face and outfit as the victim. Real professional. Expensive."

"That's nuts," Nancy said, fixing her elegantly-styled gray hair she had done in West Palm Beach just before the trip. "It also takes planning. The murders were not some spontaneous act of rage."

"I hear your shrink side emerging," Jack said. "We've analyzed everything, but not from a psychologist's point of view. Maybe you're exactly the right person to help us out right now."

"Does anyone know her motive?"

"That's what Don's pursuing. He believes she's after revenge."

"Revenge for what?"

"Not sure. Possibly her husband cheated on her. Jill's neighbor in Connecticut told Don it was well-known that her father cheated on her mother."

"Sounds like your killer is furious and acting upon that rage. Some women forgive, yet the pain and lack of trust might linger for years. Others feel too angry to stay. She's mad for her mother and for herself. But you've already surmised that, I'm sure."

"We know she's dangerous, Mom."

"Stay away from her," Patrick said.

"We're trying, Dad. It's not so simple. I didn't tell you she somehow managed to get Carrie to leave the school playground without anyone noticing. Took her for ice cream, then brought her back. Carrie likes her. Calls her 'cousin.'"

"This is much worse than you let on. What are the police doing?" Patrick said.

"Not enough. They can't find any evidence to arrest her."

"It'll happen. Don always laughs that criminals eventually make a fatal error," said Nancy.

"Mom, I didn't want to scare you. We refer to Carrie's experience as the time Jill borrowed our child. It sounds less ominous especially since she brought her right back. I still can't understand how all the teachers let this happen, claim not to have noticed."

"They're only human, dear. Don't anger anyone. You need them to be on your side, to stay alert in case there's a next time."

"Right now, we're homeschooling, but when you babysit, Jill might show up. She can be friendly and extremely engaging, totally likable. She has a nice side that would fool anyone. You've got to remember she's a killer. And she's taken to Carrie."

"Don't worry. I've got my mace," Nancy said, smoothing out her new charcoal silk top over her leggings. Why is she picking on you and your family?"

"Long story. To be continued," Jack said, happy not to reveal his misstep.

181

By now, they were at his apartment building. He double-parked, brought his parents' luggage upstairs, then scooted off to their garage.

Walking back to his building, his phone showed Jill was nearby. He searched every direction, but didn't see her. It felt creepy and his eyes started to twitch. Not a good way to instill confidence in his family so he waited outside until his body quieted down.

When the doorbell rang, Caroline didn't try to get the kids to stay put. She was tired of teaching, staying one chapter in front of the girls in each subject. The anxiety of keeping ahead of Jill also was wearing her down. She hoped her mother-in-law had enough energy to take the twins out as soon as possible, then felt guilty since Jack's parents had just arrived.

Nancy took one look at Caroline and her mothering side kicked in.

"Who wants to go play in the park?" she said, hugging the girls and telling Patrick to bring their suitcases to their room. "Who wants an orange first? Or some coconut patties?"

The girls jumped up and down as if an orange were the most valuable, longed-for treat. Jack shook his head, not believing his daughters wanted something so healthy.

"I'll put them into a plastic bag and we can take the fruit with us."

"Can Daddy come too?" Carrie said.

"And Mommy," Carly added.

"Daddy and Mommy need a rest," Nancy said. "We're going to have so much fun on our own."

Jack gave his mother an extra kiss on the cheek. She had always been his voice of reason, soothing him, encouraging him. She didn't disappoint, keeping everyone positive despite her recent flight.

"Daddy, is it okay to go alone with Grandma?" Carrie said.

Jack looked at Caroline, checking with her to see if she approved. Her smile and hug she gave Nancy were all they both needed.

"Where should we go?" Nancy said.

"I think the three of you should go to Washington Square Park." Jack said, realizing that once again, his mother made a perfect plan then managed to make it seem like it was his idea.

Once they left, Jack invited his father to join him at the gallery to view the upcoming display. Patrick was always interested in art and had been instrumental in directing his son's career. Caroline called her father to alert him that the kids would be in the park with Nancy. Then she was left with her anxiety battling with her need to rest.

# Chapter 32

"Hi there," Jill said, strolling over and sitting on a bench next to Jack's mother in the park. "I'm a friend of the family, well actually, a friend of Jack. I recognize the girls. Are you a new nanny?"

"Heavens no," Nancy said, liking the woman's warmth. "I'm Nancy, Jack's mother."

"Is he here?" Jill said, looking around.

"He's up at his gallery with my husband checking out the new exhibition. I guess I'll see you at their event in a couple of days."

"Yes. I plan to be there. For sure."

"Hello cousin," Carrie said, as soon as she saw Jill. "Did you bring ice cream?"

"We're not supposed to talk to her," Carly said to her grandmother. "Daddy says she's dangerous and we don't have any cousins."

Nancy realized they were talking to the supposed killer. She debated with herself, whether or not to stay, then took another look at the woman who seemed lovely. From her professional practice, she knew looks could be deceiving. Regardless, she decided to try to use her psychology skills to find out more, maybe even learn what Jill planned next. What could happen out in the open?

"It's okay," Nancy said to Carly. "I'll watch them. She looks nice and friendly."

At that moment, two women strolled by and sat on a nearby bench. Nancy felt comforted by having other people around.

"Would you like an orange?" she said, taking out some peeled slices she had slipped into her purse in a plastic baggie. I carried them up from Florida."

Jill accepted the beautiful fruit and sat on the bench, silently watching the girls bounce an over-sized rubber ball to each other while the sun warmed her face.

"Can we get ice cream," Carrie said.

"If you go, I want to go, too, even though we shouldn't. It's not fair that you only buy ice cream for my sister," Carly said, then turned away and made an ugly face behind Jill's back.

"I saw you," Carrie said. "You're not nice. That's why you don't get ice cream."

"Sorry girls," Nancy said. "I promised your mother you would not leave my sight. I can give this lovely lady some money and maybe she can bring ice cream here."

"Maybe in a little while," Jill said.

"How do you know Jack?" Nancy said.

"We met through his manager at the gallery. Your son is a terrific dad. I watch him and wish I still had my father. And my mother."

"Family is so important. I understand missing them," Nancy said, putting her arm around Jill. "What happened?"

"My mom committed suicide. There, I said it out loud. I usually hide the reason she died."

Nancy immediately removed her arm, shifting from soft grandma into shrink mode, listening carefully, not saying anything judgmental.

"I used to cuddle up to my mother whenever I felt sad," Jill said. "I'd share everything with my mom, well, almost everything, and would feel better. Since she ended her life, I have nobody and often feel sad and lonesome. You remind me of her."

At that moment, Nancy's phone rang. She got up to take the call. It was Caroline.

"I know Jill is with you, Nancy. I have an app on my phone that shows me where she is. Don't react to what I'm going to tell you. Keep a straight face and listen."

Nancy looked at Jill and smiled.

"Whatever you do, don't let her take the kids away. Get rid of her or take the girls home. And Don sent two undercover cops. Women. So you have help if you need it."

Nancy kept calm and nodded at the women sitting on the other bench close enough to hear her conversation. After hanging up, Nancy pressed the record button on her phone. Never having done it before, she wasn't sure it would capture the conversation she was about to continue with Jill. At least it was worth a try.

"My daughter-in-law," she said, "always worried about the girls. Now, where were we. I think you were telling me about your parents."

186

# Chapter 33

By the time Nancy burst into the apartment with the twins, Jack and Patrick had returned from mid-town. Caroline was making cappuccino and opening a package of almond dark chocolate biscotti.

"I think I have your evidence," Nancy said, not bothering to take off her jacket or sit down. "I have something with that lady's DNA thanks to Carly."

"What do you mean, Mom? How did Carly get DNA? She doesn't understand what that is," Jack said.

"I've been so worried because I know Jill was also in the park," Caroline said.

"Oh, she was there all right. She came over to me and sat down. Quite brazen, if you ask me. She recognized the girls and wanted to know if I was the new nanny. Can you imagine that? Do I look like a caretaker?"

"You look beautiful," Patrick said, ever the supportive husband.

"Then what?" Caroline said.

"We shared a bench. She was actually quite nice, friendly, chatty, very likable."

"Like a Cheshire cat, appearing and disappearing at will, often with a smile hiding her sinister side," Jack said. "Please don't engage with her again, especially when the kids are with you."

"I can't believe you let her get so close," Caroline said. "What did you talk about?"

"She told me she met Jack through your manager, Jonathan, who informed her that you're a great dad and husband," Nancy said, patting her son on the back. "That's not so bad, is it? She only had good things to say about you."

"Who cares if a murderer likes me?" Jack said, then felt badly because he was criticizing his mother and she was only visiting for a few days.

"Then what?" Jack said.

"Then I gave her some of the orange slices I brought with me for the girls."

"All very innocent, so far," said Caroline.

"She's quite pretty. And I must admit, I enjoyed having the company. I think she felt comfortable as well, because all of a sudden, she started telling me personal things one usually doesn't tell a stranger."

"You always pull deep secrets from people. I don't understand how you do it," Jack said.

"It's my shrink training. Caroline, after you called and warned me, my adrenaline kicked up. I felt like a detective and turned on the record button on my phone. I haven't had time to listen. If it worked, we might have a confession."

Jack pulled out a chair to have Nancy sit down between him and his wife. Carly climbed onto her lap. Carrie went to Patrick.

"Suddenly, Jill turned melancholy. She claimed she pushed her father off a mountain even though she loved him. She revealed this with absolutely no emotion. Evidently, he had a long-term affair and Jill decided to punish him, get revenge for the sake of her mother."

"That's so sick," Caroline said.

"Wait. It gets sicker. She also told me she drowned her husband. I think she shed a tear or two when she mentioned she drugged him first."

"You got all this on tape!" Jack said.

"I hope so. Next, Carly admired Jill's neon laces, said she wanted a pair. Right, Carly?"

"Right," said her granddaughter, smiling, looking like an innocent angel.

"Jill told her 'no, you don't. That's what I use to strangle people.'"

"No way!" Caroline said. "I'm calling my father to get here as soon as possible. He needs to hear your recording."

"Even if my phone captured all her words, she later claimed she was only kidding. I doubt it would hold up in court, but as a lawyer, you would be better able to judge. Anyway, that's not what I mean by evidence."

"There's more?" Jack said, hugging his mother.

"The girls wanted ice cream. Of course, I wouldn't let them go anywhere with the lady. Jill was very nice to Carrie. She wasn't mean to Carly, just ignored her. Carly got upset. Told her she didn't like her."

"She is mean," Carly said. "She's always mean to me."

Nancy looked at her son and Caroline, stretching out her story, milking the moment as long as possible.

"What happened next?" Jack said to his mother, trying to rush her without yelling.

"I'm getting to it. Patience," Nancy said, smiling.

"You always make us wait. I can't stand it. Spill it out," Jack said.

The girls laughed.

"Carly grabbed Jill's hand and bit her. She bit so hard Jill screamed. Other people stared at us. It was embarrassing. More important, the skin broke and Jill was bleeding."

"See, Mommy, sometimes biting is good," Carly said, then made a face at her sister.

"No!" said Caroline. "Biting people is never good. We'll talk about it later."

"What did you do next?" Jack said, punching his dad playfully and nodding as if his mother was their hero and he knew it all along.

"The only thing I could think of. I took out my handkerchief and wrapped it around Jill's hand. She was in no mood to accept my kindness. Her gorgeous eyes turned to daggers. Her voice became a hiss. It was frightening to see the transformation. She tore off the handkerchief, threw it at me and left. It's amazing how quickly she can walk in her extra-high high-heeled boots."

"Tell me you have the bloody handkerchief," Caroline said. "That's all we might need to determine if her DNA matches the skin under Blondie's nails."

Nancy dug into a side pouch of her handbag and pulled out the soiled handkerchief, careful to touch only a tiny part of one corner.

Caroline ran to get fresh gloves she uses to wash the dishes, then put the handkerchief inside a zip-lock plastic bag.

"My father is going to love you for this," Caroline said.

"He can thank Carly."

"Please don't praise her. Biting is not something we condone. We're trying so hard to get her to use words instead of her teeth when she gets upset."

Jack felt his daughter deserved some sort of recognition. He was about to argue with his wife, then decided to remain quiet, simply putting his arm around Carly.

# Chapter 34

"While Jack and Caroline sat in the kitchen finishing their cappuccino, his foot was shaking under the table. Caroline alternated between taking sips and blowing air out of her mouth. After an uncomfortable silence, Jack looked straight at his wife.

"I have a confession to make," he said.

"I don't want to hear your confession. Not now. Not while there's so much going on about Jill and Carrie and your parents staying in our apartment. I'm so glad they took the girls out again. I need some quiet time."

"Now that we're alone, I need to tell you something," he said.

"If you tell me will it make you feel better?"

"Yes. We've never kept secrets and this has been bothering me for a few weeks."

"After you tell me, how will the information make me feel?"

"Terrible, I guess," he said, his eyes twitching for the second time in one day.

"Then save it, because I already feel awful."

Caroline suspected Jack had cheated with Jill, though she wasn't sure. She had a reasonable doubt and as long as there was doubt, she decided she could pretend he was innocent. Then there was the gun she had found.

Maybe all he wanted to divulge was how it came into his pocket.

"Is it about a gun?" she said.

He nodded, not opening his mouth, wondering how he could tell her about the pistol without mentioning he took it from Jill's apartment.

"I love you so much," he said, leaning toward her, wanting to hug her.

"Hold on," she said, putting up her hand. "I love you, too. Now that we got that out of the way, tell me about the gun. Only the gun. I can't handle anything else now."

"I stole it."

"You stole a gun! What's wrong with you? Did you take it from a gun store? They must have cameras all over the place."

"No. I stole it from Jill."

"You stole a firearm from the supposed murderer! How was that possible? Is it a legal weapon?"

"It's a handgun and I have no idea if she had it legally."

"Let me get this right. You're telling me you stole a pistol from the woman you think strangled the blonde girl in your art gallery. Did you steal it in London when we were all there?"

"No. Before. Before we went overseas."

Caroline put her head in her hands. Jack tried to rub her shoulders. She pushed him away.

"I left it in my blazer," he said. "The one you sent to the cleaners, so I think you found the gun. You're just making me suffer."

Caroline opted not to acknowledge she had the firearm.

"How did you get this weapon?" she said.

"It's a long story."

"Give me the short version before your parents come back with the girls."

Jack sat next to her, head hanging, mouth pinched closed.

"Does that mean you won't tell me?"

"No. Give me a minute. I was in the Downtown Bar and Grill with Jonathan. He's sort-of friendly with Jill so she came over to talk to us."

"The manager of your New York gallery is friendly with the woman we believe to be a murderer. And you've known this for how long?"

"Your dad knows about this. He already interrogated Jonathan. Turns out they're not really friends. Don made him try to get a sample of her DNA to compare to the skin under Blondie's nails. I guess she's too slippery to let that happen."

"I thought I was working on this case with my father. How come you know more than I do?" she said, making a mental note to call her dad.

Jack shook his head.

"Just get to the gun part," Caroline said. "How the hell did you take it from Jill?"

"She didn't see me take it. Her handbag fell. I picked it up. It felt heavy so I looked inside."

"You looked inside a stranger's handbag! Are you crazy? Didn't she see you?"

"No. She was nursing a drink."

It was a lie, yet Jack felt it was believable. He was beginning to feel comfortable with his confession, though he knew he shouldn't, especially since Don knew the truth.

"Curiosity can be dangerous," Caroline said, pushing her husband to continue.

"I panicked when I saw the gun and slipped it into my pocket. I'm not sure why," Jack said. "Where's the pistol? What did you do with it?"

"I'm not ready to share that information. I need it. You can't take it back."

"What do you need the gun for?" Jack said, becoming alarmed.

"To shoot Jill. Pow," she said, pointing her index finger as if pulling a trigger.

"Now which one of us is crazy? You don't know how to shoot. You can hurt yourself. And you don't have a permit to carry a weapon."

"I know. It's a felony. If I get caught, I could go to jail, or lose my right to practice law. If that happens, I'll figure out how to fight it. Meanwhile, I'm learning to shoot. I already had my first lesson. Legally, I'm only allowed to use a rifle. I hope the pistol will be similar enough to do the job."

"Let your father capture this lunatic. He knows what he's doing."

"After she kidnaps Carrie again? Do you think I'll just sit around while everyone else walks in circles knowing this woman is out there, always near us."

"I want her out of our lives, too. But I also want you to stay safe. There has to be a better way than you risking your life in a duel."

"No duel. I intend to shoot her in the back."

"Wow. What happened to the sweet young girl I met in high school?"

"She became a mother whose child is threatened. What would you do if I give you the gun? Return it to Jill?"

"Of course not. I'd dump it in the Hudson River, get rid of my error and the possibility that if you use it, we might be in a worse mess than we are now."

"You can have it after Jill is dead. That's a promise."

"Swear you won't have a shoot-out with her. I need you."

"Right. You love me and need me. I love you and need to get rid of a deadly threat to our family. And you better not tell my father I have this gun."

# Chapter 35

"Mom, it's hard having my in-laws stay with us, even though I've known them since I was a kid. I clean up then clean again, wondering if Jack's mother thinks I'm a good enough wife."

Caroline was in Martha's kitchen helping to cook her mother's famous lasagna.

"You've been married for over ten years, publicly, thirteen since your elopement. You and Nancy should be used to each other by now. Besides, you have a housekeeper once a week. You can always blame a dust ball or two on her."

"That's not the point. I also feel like I have to justify how I spend my time. I don't want her to think I'm lazy or not doing my fair share with the family since I'm not working."

"Taking care of the twins is work, especially with home schooling. And you're helping your father solve the look-alike doll killings."

"It's not a real job. It's for Daddy so I can do no wrong. To be honest, I participate when it's convenient," she said, combining sausage with chop meat before placing the mixture in a frying pan.

"Honey, Jack's parents adore you, have since high school. At this point, who cares? You're married, you've had your kids and your in-laws moved far away. I bet Nancy needs your approval more than you need hers. Be kind. Make the best of a short visit. Besides, that bloody handkerchief she kept might be exactly what the police need to convict. It could turn out that Nancy is our heroine.

Caroline whipped ricotta with an egg, then opened a package of shredded mozzarella cheese to blend with the ricotta while her mother chopped fresh basil.

"Your mouth is a tight scowl," Martha said, "like whenever you got a grade you didn't like. It was the foreshadowing of an all-out attack on your studies until you earned what you felt you deserved. Your face makes me feel like a storm is about to break. What else is bothering you?"

Caroline sighed.

"Carly is a biter and thinks she's a hero because of it. Carrie is enamored with a killer who pops up at random and has targeted Jack who believes he can calm us both by drinking tea and eating dark chocolate. My father-in-law takes credit for all of Jack's success and my mother-in-law is a perfectionist who does everything better than I can ever hope to do. She's in my home, sees everything and because she's a shrink, her visit is making me crazy."

"Sounds normal to me. Well, not the killer part."

"Our life is not normal."

"It's normal not to be normal, whatever that means. Just breathe, honey. Take a moment to slow down. Try the yoga Pranayama you attempted to teach me and the alternate nostril practice thing. It makes me laugh, but you claim it helps."

"I'm surprised you remember," Caroline said, taking a deep breath.

"Actually, a friend, Steve, tried to get me to participate in a yoga class at the gym you sent me to with your father. It's still not for me."

"You went back to the gym."

"Don and I have been going together. At first, we hated it, then it became fun. Now tell your mama what's really causing so much stress," Martha said, pouring Chianti into two glasses."

"Jack and I have been fighting," Caroline said, taking more than a sip of her wine. "I told him I found the gun he was hiding from me in the pocket of his blazer."

"Good, two secrets, gone."

"Yes, but I'm not sure I trust him."

"Ah. Trust. Are you asking me, of all people, to comment on trusting a man? I believe we had this discussion already."

By now both women were layering pans with lasagna noodles, meat, sauce and cheese, organizing enough for the whole family that would be sharing the dish along with a giant salad and crunchy garlic bread paired with some good red wine.

"Do you think Jack is having an affair?" Martha said.

"No. But he might have had a one-night fling with Jill. I'm not sure."

"Ask him."

"I don't want to know."

"Then assume the best."

"How did you find out about Dad cheating?"

"He made excuses to go out alone, then came home late, often. He became overprotective of his computer and phone. Didn't want me to see messages. Of course, I found ways to check."

"Now that we know Jill is targeting Jack, even if she leaves a message on his phone, it doesn't mean they had sex, does it?"

"Ask him," Martha said, again.

"I don't want to know."

"So you said. Twice."

"Did you ask Dad if he was having an affair?"

"Yes. He admitted it right away. Seemed relieved to confess and promised to end the relationship. He went to therapy. Sometimes I joined him. It was all very painful."

"How did you two get back? How did you find a way to trust him again?"

"Like I told you the last time you questioned me, I'm not sure I do, yet. Remember, we're together, separately. Maybe the trust will come later. Maybe never. Right now, we're in sync, even better than before. It feels great."

"Should Jack and I go to therapy?"

"Some people think it never hurts. Others believe it's best not to stir things up. You don't even know if he had sex with anyone else. You were so young when you discovered each other. If he did, maybe he only wanted a one-time experience. That's different from an affair."

"It would still hurt. I don't want to have to throw him out. I love him. The girls love him. I love our balanced life together."

"If you're lucky, life is long. Good marriages leave room for mistakes," Martha said. "At least I'm trying to buy into that."

"Mom! An out-of-marriage sexual relationship is more than a mistake. I can't be so forgiving."

"I understand. Right now, you have a bigger problem than infidelity."

"You mean the look-alike doll that has Jack's face."

"I bet Jill plans to strike at the art opening, just like she did in London. Your father is going to flood the place with cops."

"Jill already told Nancy she plans to attend. I'm going to be there with my new-found pistol."

"Caroline, I know, better than most, you can be headstrong. Don't do anything foolish. Your father has Jack's back and yours. He'll be at the gallery. He'll be carrying a gun. Just promise me you won't drink anything. She might lace a beverage with a drug."

# Chapter 36

"My mom and I made lasagna for tonight," Caroline said, over an early cup of coffee with her husband before his parents and the kids got up. "We're all going over to her place."

"I'm glad you're getting help with the cooking," Jack said. "It's been tough for you, and I appreciate everything you're doing to make sure Mom and Dad have a good time."

He reached across the table to hold her hand. She let him, enjoying a bit of private time together.

It was a day before the opening of the artist's exhibit and Caroline still had not confronted her husband about his cheating. She did not have the courage to face an honest answer if it turned out to be true. The conversation with her mother had not been as helpful as Caroline had hoped. She would have to rely upon her own instincts.

Jack was nervous with the usual worries about introducing a new contemporary painter. Add the fear of Jill and it was not the right time to discuss anything. He needed all the loving support his wife could muster.

While they were sitting at the table, Caroline jumped up, went to the bookcase in the den and brought back their wedding album.

"It's not our anniversary. Why are we looking at these photos now?"

"With your parents here, I thought they might like to see them and remember what a wonderful day it was," Caroline said, not telling him she was using the photos as a diversion to avoid discussing any of their crazy problems.

"You were such a beautiful bride," Jack said. "Both times. Too bad we don't have an album from our elopement."

"Not to worry. That day is etched into my brain and I can see us any time I want."

"If you really want to be nostalgic, let's look at our high school yearbook," he said. "That's when our life together really started."

"I forgot what a romantic you are," she said, then returned to the den to retrieve the book and a few other albums.

"We were so young. Look how much hair you had. I think I fell for your dark wavy curls first, or maybe your dark eyes, much like Carrie's."

"You always had blondish hair. My sweet Caroline. Well, not always sweet," he said with a laugh. "You were so sure of yourself. I envied your self-confidence."

"And you had the best smile. I always felt at home next to you. Look what you wrote," she said, pointing to his photo in the yearbook. "Now and forever."

"I meant it then and I mean it today," he said, bending over to kiss her. "It's too bad that with all the new technology, our kids might not have albums, just flash drives, phones and computers filled with photos."

"Speaking of flash drives, I could swear I found four in Jill's apartment. My father says I'm mistaken. He claims there were only three."

"He ought to know," Jack said, grateful his father-in-law did not reveal that there was evidence of himself with Jill.

"Maybe the fourth item I remember was the sound piece we heard in the car."

"What was on it?" he asked, scared of the answer.

"Jill seemed to be conversing with foreigners about a shipment of something. It was unclear."

"What do you mean?"

"There was so much static, it was hard to tell if the voices were male or female or all the same. Daddy says it repeats in a loop so it's not real. He thinks she created the conversation to scare people, like his client, Silver Fox, the one who was strangled in the Downtown Bar and Grill."

Jack turned dark. "Are we reviewing our life through photos because you think I'm going to be strangled with a pair of long neon shoelaces tomorrow?"

Caroline shivered. It was exactly what she was worried about, but decided to hide her anxiety. Jack had enough on his own.

"No. I thought your parents might like to see the albums while they're visiting."

"The good news is that I haven't received a look-alike doll," Jack said. "No doll. No murder, right?"

"I hope so. Even if you receive one, Daddy won't let Jill get you."

Jack nodded, though unconvinced. "If the London art opening is any indication of how Jill works, I bet a doll gets delivered to the gallery tomorrow."

"If it does, what should we do?"

"Not accept the package is one option," he said, "and not go to the restroom alone."

They shook their heads simultaneously.

"I know that's not going to work. They're not even funny ideas," Jack said. "I'm in no shape to make light of the situation."

"Thankfully, Dad's going to bring in plainclothes police. In London, we were on our own. Here, we'll be surrounded by professionals who can help us."

"Remind me to put their names on the guest list so they'll be allowed in," Jack said.

"What if Jill shows up incognito? She's done that so many times. List or no list, I bet she finds a way to get in."

"Honey, you're creeping me out."

"Do you want to call off the event?" Caroline said.

"It's too late. The artist arranged his schedule to be here tomorrow and so many people have confirmed. Jonathan and Oliver are finally working as a team. They bought ads and managed to convince a few reporters to show up."

"And I bought a new dress," Caroline said. "A black satin strapless thing I won't show you until tomorrow. Will you also wear all black?"

"That's easy. Anything else to please you, babe?"

"Well, since you asked, I have another idea. We can pretend that tomorrow is the day Jill gets shot. That way we can look forward to the party with joy rather than fear. Tomorrow will mark the day we are able to get our lives back to normal."

"You're dreaming."

"I have a premonition."

"As long as you don't do the shooting, it sounds fine to me. Though you have the gun you found in my pocket, you promised not to use it."

"I did no such thing. I told you I would give it back to you once Jill is dead."

# Chapter 37

"We're pretty sure Jill's going to show up tonight," Don said, in a private meeting in Jack's office about an hour before clients were expected to arrive for the opening of the new art exhibit. "Caroline and I are tracking her whereabouts on our phones."

"If we see Jill, what should we do?" said Oliver, who had flown in from London to help run the event.

"Stay calm and look to Don for advice," Jack said, with a quivering smile that barely covered his intense fear. "He's in charge of protection."

"Since the gallery is on the third floor," Don said, "I hired two women to stay in the lobby and direct visitors to the elevator. They're undercover police, tougher than they look. And they are armed."

Jack also hired guards his father-in-law had recommended, "just in case." They were in uniform. Hopefully, the guests would think it was standard procedure for a Madison Avenue event. Nobody beyond the immediate family and staff had any idea about a just-in-case scenario.

"It's almost six o'clock. Last chance for any questions," Don said.

Everyone kept quiet, including Caroline who opted to play the role of supportive wife and daughter.

"Off to mingle, everyone. And stay alert," Don said, leaving the office and declining a flute of champagne from a waitress carrying a tray from room to room.

Caroline left the office to wander. She looked stunning in her strapless short dress with matching long gloves. She knew she was a tad overdressed, perhaps looking more appropriate for the Metropolitan opera, but didn't care. The dress made her feel good and she needed all the good feelings she could find.

She hoped others assumed the gloves were part of the look she had chosen, although she wore them to cover her fingerprints in case she needed to use the gun she carried in her purse. She completed her outfit with extravagantly expensive, sparkling designer sneakers rather than the five-inch heels she preferred to show off her legs. The sneakers would enable her to creep up on Jill and to run, if need be.

"See that guy over there in the purple shirt," Don said to Caroline in a whisper. "He's a cop. Don't stare, but the man near the wine table in a suit is also a cop. And the guy sitting next to Jonathan at the check-in table at the front door is one of mine."

"How many did you bring in?"

"Six undercover not counting the two by the elevator and the guards in uniform. They've all seen Jill's photo and have been briefed. They'll be on the look-out for her or anything 'out of the ordinary,' whatever that might mean."

Looking around, Caroline was relieved to know there were plainclothes police mingling amongst the guests. Then she spotted her husband. His eyes kept twitching; his body trembled. It was not a good way for the owner of the gallery to present himself. She moved toward him, grabbing his hand in support. Don followed.

"We need a guard in each bathroom," Jack said to Don while holding Caroline's gloved fingers. "Can you assign two more people or do I need to ask the cops downstairs?"

"I'll handle it," Don said.

Jack left them, circled back to the crowd, shaking people's hands, welcoming clients he knew, introducing his artist to new faces, flitting from one to another.

"Easy, Jack," Oliver said. "Try to stand in one place for a minute before scooting off to someone else. You're making your entire team uneasy."

"I know, but I can't help it. Thanks for upping the décor. You have a flair. And Jonathan did well with the drinks and the caterer," Jack said, slapping Oliver on the back before zipping off to welcome and talk up a good collector who had just walked in.

During the past days Oliver had sensed there was a rift between Jonathan and their boss, though Oliver didn't have a clue as to why. At least the New York manager had been pleasant to work with, implementing Oliver's suggestions to bring in some large lush plants, where to place the hors d'oeuvres and set-up extra lighting.

He was not surprised that the attending crowd was a little less edgy, a bit older and a touch less exciting than the one he had assembled in London. On the other hand, they might have more disposable income to invest in art. Jonathan had done a good job reaching out.

Just then, one of the guards came up to Jack. "There's a Harley parked on the side of the building near the loading dock. It's the only vehicle there. Should we find a cop to issue a ticket, have it towed, or look away?"

Jack immediately found Don.

"What should we do?"

"Ignore it," Don said. "She's here, as expected, probably incognito, maybe wearing a colorful wig or one of her other costumes. Signal me if you see her."

Caroline, holding a glass of white wine in her black-gloved hand, watched her husband and her father, then circulated. The looks and smiles she got from the young men milling about made her feel sexy which normally would make her smile. Today, she couldn't enjoy the attention. She was too aware of the gun in her purse and a citrus fragrance that filled the air.

She watched her mother-in-law standing in her pastel dress that worked in Florida, but was a bit too toned down for this crowd. No matter. All Caroline hoped was that Jill did not come by even though the suspected murderer had told Nancy she would.

Caroline remembered she wasn't supposed to drink. She abandoned her wine on the newly set-up bar, searched around, then saw a short, thin person in a UPS outfit carrying a package that was about 18 inches or so. She wondered why Jonathan didn't sign for the delivery and how the UPS person managed to get into the gallery. Caroline looked more carefully and realized it was Jill.

Maybe she had slipped in through the side door by the stairwell.

It was too late to send a guard to cover that area. The enemy was already inside. Caroline exhaled, glad to be getting her chance to eliminate the danger to her family, not sure how she would pull it off with 100 or so people milling about.

"Don't be alarmed," Don said, coming over with Jack and putting his arm around his daughter, not noticing that she was calm compared to her husband who was shaking and easily flustered.

Jonathan also appeared, interested in talking to the UPS person he had let slip by at the reception desk. Up close, he realized it was Jill and didn't want to be responsible for anything terrible that might happen. At the same time, he wanted to warn her that the place was loaded with cops. He'd alert Don after she left.

When Jack accepted the package, the UPS person winked at him. Jill's excessive citrus perfume filled the air. He panicked, hurrying with the box to his office, leaving his wife, Don and Jonathan. By the time they followed him, Jack had already locked the door and tore the delivery open. To his horror, there was the look-alike doll everyone had been anticipating. At first, he was going to tell the cops, but that might cause alarm amongst the guests and destroy his event. Then he decided not to scare Caroline and just get the doll out of the gallery.

He opened his office door and peeked out. The UPS person was gone. Don and Caroline were hovering, waiting for him. He showed them the doll, then tucked it under his blazer.

"Whatever happens, just remember I love you," he said, as Jonathan started to yell something about Jill getting away. In the confusion, Jack quickly ran past everyone, past the oversized oil paintings on bright white walls with special lighting, past the people milling about in the main gallery and slipped out of the party.

Jack's first impulse was to take the elevator to another floor, but guests were still arriving and the lifts were occupied. Instead, he raced through the side door to the stairwell to climb up two flights and leave the look-alike on the landing. He wanted to separate himself from it and its ominous message as soon as possible. No doll, no murder, he hoped.

# Chapter 38

Jack's terror pushed him faster. As he raced up the stairs, he looked at the doll again, horrified at how much it looked like him, wondering what it would look like inside a coffin. Then his brain cleared and he raced up, two steps at a time, using his free hand to hold the banister and propel himself faster, his black leather shoes making a soft noise on the steps.

On the staircase below, he heard someone following him. When he reached the fifth-floor landing he stopped, out of breath, terrified.

*How the hell did I get here?* Jack wondered, plastered against the wall of the inside stairwell a few floors above his art gallery. He was still clutching the doll that looked exactly like him complete with skinny jeans, a white shirt and navy blazer. Most disturbing was a miniature pistol in the jacket pocket. Everyone else who had received a mini-me doll had been murdered. He could hear someone breathing close by, but there was no place for him to go.

The gun he had stolen from Jill's apartment was gone. He still had no idea what his wife had done with it. It didn't matter since he didn't know how to shoot. Despite the fear it had produced, he found himself remembering the first time he wrapped his fingers around the weapon. Thinking about the cold, hard metal drove his mind back to the evening his nightmare began.

"Jill, I know you're there," he said, assuming she had followed him to the stairs. He hoped his voice sounded stronger than he felt, his damp hair flattened against his sweaty forehead. "Turn yourself in. It's the only way out."

"Not true. You die and I'm out," she said, climbing higher, then pointing her gun at him.

Her voice echoed in the stairwell. He could hear classical music drifting from his art gallery and realized nobody would hear him scream.

"I have your gun. The one I stole the first time we were together," he said, keeping his hand in his jacket pocket, trying to sound confident with his lie. If you come any closer, I'll shoot you." He hoped she didn't know he was bluffing.

Jill laughed. "Tell me Jack, is it loaded?"

She was always a few steps ahead of him, even at the bar when he thought he was picking her up, she had been toying with him, setting him up for a fall. He felt like a child playing with older, mean kids who knew how to torment him, only this was lethal.

While he tried to think of ways to delay the inevitable, he remembered his elopement and his later, formal wedding. If he survived, he promised himself to be a better husband, a better father, a better son. He would do the dishes every night. He would help make the bed, hell, he'd make it on his own and he would take out the garbage without being reminded. Most of all, he would never cheat again.

"Jack," Jill said in a sing song voice. "You've gotten awfully quiet."

Thanks to her phone, Caroline knew Jill was on the stairs. She raced to the stairwell and stopped when she reached the landing to the fifth-floor staircase where she saw her husband above the killer. If Caroline crept up a few more steps, she would have a direct line to her target, but Jill would probably see her.

Caroline's hand was shaking, a complete surprise to her since she felt a strange peace. Since Jill was armed, Caroline understood that if she missed, this beautiful lunatic would shoot her and Jack and turn her innocent children into orphans. Would her mother and father fight Nancy and Patrick for custody or would they take turns? Perhaps the kids would be split, one child for each set of grandparents.

*Stop it,* she told herself.

Caroline tried to muster the courage she had in the beginning of the evening. It seemed so far away. The time lapse was making her crazy. Then she got a grip. She'd been planning this moment ever since Jill borrowed Carrie and showed she was a danger to their family. That woman had to be eliminated. Now!

When Jack left the art show, Don had followed. He could see Jill almost together with Jack on the landing, their eyes glued to one another. Once again, his age was slowing him down. To complicate the situation, he saw his daughter in the middle of the staircase a few steps above him. It was all too spontaneous and without a plan, he was less confident than normal.

Jonathan had also followed, but remained at the bottom of the staircase. He still considered warning Jill that there were other people around besides Jack. He just didn't know how he could do that without endangering everyone. Then he remembered she's a murderer after his boss. He became paralyzed, unable to leave, while unable to help.

Jack needed to think quickly. Despite his adrenaline, his mind was fuzzy, so he tried to keep the conversation going, wanting to stall for more time, hoping a good idea would fill his head that was gripped with fear.

"Why did you send me a doll?" Jack said, in a weak voice.

"Just a gift before you die."

"I get it, but why a look-alike doll? You can kill someone without an expensive forewarning."

"Expense is no problem. I have money."

"That explains nothing."

"If I tell, you'll think it's silly."

"There's nothing silly about us sitting in a stairwell pointing guns at each other."

"Okay, when I was little, my parents bought me a doll that was supposed to look like me. It was generic. I was so disappointed, even though I kept it my whole life. When I got older, my father found a place that made dolls for the entertainment industry as well as for the rich and famous."

"So, he made one for you."

"An exact replica. He gave it to me in Colorado, just before he had his fatal accident. I was touched that he was so thoughtful. At the same time, I was angry it took him so long to do something nice for me."

While Jill talked, Caroline took out her gun from her purse, then crept up another few steps. Don watched, opting not to reveal his presence.

"I was already an adult," Jill said, "too old to play with dolls, though I really liked it. He showed me a doll he had made for himself and we sat on the mountain, enjoying them together. It was one of my best moments with him."

"Was this just before he fell?"

"Just before he died. After, I threw his doll down to be with him, to keep him company. You think this is ridiculous, right?"

Jack thought it was insane, but opted to humor her.

"It's strange, or at the very least, unusual. I still don't get why you went through the trouble of getting all your victims dolls."

"It was fun. Life should include some fun, don't you agree?"

"You think dolls and murder are fun?" he said, trying to understand her reasoning.

"After I got mine, I decided everyone should have such a special gift once in a lifetime. I can't buy the world dolls, but I can give my victims a moment of joy before the end."

She sounded absurd, but this was not the time to argue.

"Did you and Jonathan have a bet about me?" he said, shifting the conversation away from murder.

"You'll have to ask Jonathan. Nice guy. Adores you, by the way. Now, I think it's time to stop our banter."

"What do you want?" Jack said, in a panic, trying to stall the inevitable.

"I'm so glad you asked. I want Carrie. You have two girls. Give me one and I'm out of your life."

"You're even crazier than I thought."

"It's really quite simple. You give me Carrie or you die."

"There's no way I'm giving you one of my daughters."

"Then you'll have to shoot me to get out of here alive."

"The gallery is swarming with cops," he said. "Even if you kill me, you'll never make it out of here alive."

# Chapter 39

Caroline inched closer to Jill, holding the pistol in one hand and resting her other hand on her purse that was draped across her shoulder. Her brain flashed to the mandatory safety course she had taken at the rifle range. She remembered no alcoholic beverages before or during a shoot. Too late. She already had a taste of wine at the art opening. Then she recalled no running, jumping or climbing with a loaded firearm. Here she was, climbing stairs. Third to come to mind was to dress correctly. She wasn't hunting outdoors, so who cared if she wore her strapless little black dress. Her small, fancy shoulder bag on her bare shoulder dug into her and made her movements awkward. At least she had traded her Christian Louboutin 5-inch heels for sneakers.

Caroline tried to control her breathing. She could see Jack and Jill above her, Jack on the landing and Jill just below him, exchanging verbal barbs. Looking down the stairs, she was stunned to see her father coming up. Behind him, near the bottom, was Jonathan. If Jill turned her head, she would see everyone.

"Shh," she motioned with her finger on her lips, not willing to say anything for fear the sound would alert Jill to their presence. She had been so careful to stay concealed when Jack left the party, following him to the stairwell, watching him climb to the next floors while clutching that ominous doll. No surprise her dad had seen them, too.

Jack still had his eyes locked on Jill. He had no idea his wife or anyone else was on the stairs. He thought he was alone with his killer, about to be shot. He leaned back against the wall, then sank to the floor.

Caroline's adrenaline kicked up a notch when she heard Jill ask for Carrie. It gave her the courage she had started to lose. Then her dad spoiled everything.

"I'm right behind you, Jill," Don said, booming above the sound of music floating up from the gallery. "There's no way you can escape, with or without killing Jack. If you love Carrie, let him go. Let her have her father."

"Very funny, Mr. Detective. You really think I don't have a plan. If you think that I'm going to listen to you, then you have no idea who I am."

"I know exactly who you are," Caroline said, shouting. "You're the crazy bitch who's trying to destroy my family. Well, surprise, I have your gun and I know how to use it. You can be sure it's loaded and I'm going to pull the trigger unless you let Jack leave."

"Shit," Jack said softly, understanding that Jill now knew he was unarmed.

"Well, well. Movies I've seen usually have two or three people on a staircase. Looks like we have a family reunion," Jill said. "Where's Nancy? She's my favorite. I saw her at the party. The other grandma must be with the kids."

"You see Jack's above you and we're below you," Don said, pointing his gun at Jill. "You can't escape. It's time for you to give up and let Jack go."

"If Caroline has my gun, then Jack has nothing in his pocket besides his hand. Makes him an even easier target."

"Shoot him and you'll die," said Caroline, also pointing her pistol at Jill.

"I'd like to spare Jack. He was the nicest of all my pick-ups, and I've come to adore Carrie. Shocking isn't it, that I can care for anyone."

"Not shocking. Not at all," said Jonathan in as loud a voice as he could muster.

"Jonathan. You're here!" Jill said, seeing him at the bottom of the stairs. "Are you aiming a gun at me, too?"

"I wanted to warn you about all the cops," he said.

"Sounds like I do have a friend. Makes me glad about my arrangement."

"What arrangement?"

"You'll find out later."

"What the fuck are you doing here?" Don said to Jonathan without taking his eyes off Jill.

"Jill loaned me money. She's been nice to me. If she promises not to harm any of you and to leave Carrie alone, can't you let her go. I'll watch her."

"If you believe that she'd honor her promise, you must be as crazy as she is," Don said. "Or just plain naïve. Stick to art, Jonathan. You'll live a lot longer."

"If I let Jack go, what'll you do, Don?" Jill said, still pointing her gun at Jack.

"Take you into custody. You're wanted for at least two murders that have nothing to do with Jack. I have to bring you to the police."

"Jail time, right?"

"They won't hold you long. We have no proof against you."

"What about the damn bloody handkerchief I threw at Nancy. Big mistake. My father would be disappointed in me. Not part of the plan."

"It gave us a sample of your DNA that matches the skin under the fingernails of Blondie. Believe it or not, that's still not anything more than circumstantial evidence. The poor girl could have scratched you before she went into the loo. Someone else could have strangled her in the bathroom, though we have no other suspects."

"You make it sound so easy. I get arrested for murder. All evidence is circumstantial. The case gets dismissed."

"You got it. I'll make sure the court assigns the best defense attorney the government can provide."

"I can hire my own lawyer. I don't need a government handout."

As Jack listened to the conversation, he was glad to have Don backing him up. Despite all the guns, he began to believe he had a chance to come out of this alive.

"Do we have a deal?" Don said to Jill. "I'll even sweeten it with a box of chocolate chip cookies."

"Sorry, Don."

"Let me bring you in. I have no other choice."

"I do," said Caroline. "I'm a civilian. You see my gun and I have a choice. Let my husband walk down to us unharmed. We'll leave and then you can disappear."

"Sounds nice, but I don't believe you."

Jack wished he were religious. He sure could use a prayer or two at this moment, but all he mustered was a mantra that somehow his wife would be saved, promising whatever spiritual savior might exist that he would never stray again.

For a while everyone was silent. The quiet seemed deafening. Then a shot rang out, hitting the ceiling light, plunging them into total darkness before a second shot blasted into its target.

# Chapter 40

When the stairwell became dark, Caroline screamed. Jonathan groaned. Jack almost wet his pants while his eyes twitched and his heart pounded. Jill remained silent.

"Jill, what are you up to?" Don said. "Did you fire to let us know you're armed? We get it."

There was no answer.

"What's your plan?" he said, aiming his gun where her voice had come from. "What happens next?"

There was no comment from the beautiful lunatic.

"Jack," Caroline said softly, trying to control her panic. "I can't see you. Are you okay?"

"I think so," he said.

Caroline let out a long breath of relief.

"Dad," she said." Did you shoot the second shot?"

"No," Don said, moving up the stairs to be closer to his daughter.

"I wanted to kill her. I wanted to be the one who got rid of her. I don't know why I waited."

"You did the right thing. We'll discuss how you got a gun later."

"Jonathan," Don said, turning toward the bottom of the staircase. "Do you have a weapon?"

"Are you fucking mad?" he said, curling up to the banister at the base of the staircase, as close to a fetal position as he could manage.

Don left Caroline and inched his way up toward Jill, his pistol still in his hand.

"Jesus Christ. She planted a bullet right through her heart!"

One hand was still wrapped around her gun. Don lifted her other hand and took her pulse.

"She's gone," he said, then closed her aquamarine eyes.

The four of them remained quiet for a minute, not in prayer for the dead or respect for the person who had taken her life. They were stunned. Jack broke the silence, flailing his arms in the air.

"I have to…I have to…I have to…"

"I shouldn't let you leave, but you have to get your wife and her illegal gun out of here," Don said to his son-in-law, taking charge. "Bring her home to be with the kids, then Martha can come back to the gallery with you."

Jack sat paralyzed on the floor, placing his head in his hands.

"Get up and get out of here so I can alert the police, but you must return. It's your event and the cops will want to question you."

"Dad, everyone at the party saw me. They all know I was here. Won't they want to question me, too?" Caroline said.

"That's okay. You made an appearance, then went home to relieve your mother from babysitting."

"I want to stay to support Jack. I didn't do anything wrong."

"How are you going to explain your weapon? Carrying an unlicensed pistol is a felony. If I put my job ahead of family, I'd take it from you and turn you in right now. Go. Both of you. Get out of here and get rid of the weapon."

"What about me?" Jonathan said, continuing to hug the banister as if it could provide a needed hug back.

"Get inside the gallery. If anyone questions you, send them to me. The less you say, the better."

Jonathan tried to leave, but his feet wouldn't obey his brain. Don walked down the stairs, put his arm under Jonathan's shoulder, pulled his fingers off the railing and lifted him to a standing position.

"Go to the gallery," he said, a little more gently than he felt. "You're okay. We're all okay."

"I heard Jill kill herself. She was so beautiful. I can't chit chat with customers right now."

"You can, and you will," Don said, then turned toward Jack.

"I saw her do it," Jack said. "Even though the light was gone, I was close enough to watch her turn her gun toward her chest. I can't get the moment out of my brain…the sound, the blood. Maybe I should have tried to stop her. That's what a good person would have done, but I was scared she'd kill me."

"It happened too fast for any of us to do anything," Don said. "And as long as she was alive, we were all in danger."

"I guess she got off lightly," Jack said. "After the turmoil she put my family through, and killing Blondie, she deserved to be emotionally tortured at a trial and then rot in jail."

"Stop wasting your time thinking and give me the doll. I'll tell Smith it was delivered here. You panicked, ran to the stairs trying to hide. I saw you leave and followed. Jill zipped out ahead of me. I tried to get her to surrender. The rest the police can determine on their own."

"It's all true," Caroline said. "Any one of us will say the same thing. With the pistol clenched in Jill's hand and her fingerprints all over it, none of us will be accused of anything."

"I wanted to be the one who shot her," Caroline said, again. "When she took her own life, she took that away from me."

By now, Jack had gathered enough strength to walk down past Jill's body to be with his wife.

"Jack, you'll be questioned," Don said. "Since you were unarmed and the target, you'll have no problem. Take my daughter and her gun out of here so I can alert the police. They probably noticed I'm not in the gallery and already realized something is up. Hurry and get out of here."

Outside, Jack took off his suit jacket and put it around his wife who was shivering. Jill's motorcycle was still parked at the side of the building. One cop was writing a ticket. A second cop waved to Jack, recognizing him as the owner of the gallery where the party was taking place.

"I'm afraid one of your guests is going to be upset to discover this ticket."

"I doubt it," Jack said, hailing a cab, glad that the homicide police had not yet arrived and the traffic cop was unaware of the activity in and around the gallery.

"I hear sirens. We got out just in time," Caroline said, gulping air, then trying to steady her breathing.

Once in the cab, she looked out the window, angry at herself for not shooting.

"Where are we going?" she said, noticing they were too far west to be on the way to their apartment.

"We're going to take a detour, a short walk along the Hudson River. A brief moment to collect ourselves before facing the rest of the evening."

"You pick an odd moment to become romantic. Is that absolutely necessary?"

"Absolutely," he said.

In what seemed like a nano second, they were strolling along the water's edge, his arm around her, a couple in love if anyone happened to see them. When they reached a point that was close to the river, Jack instructed Caroline to open her purse.

"Take out the gun," he said. "Toss it into the water, then turn and kiss me."

Caroline followed his directions, glad he was stepping up and taking charge, praying there wouldn't be a huge splash. Somehow, the weapon slipped quietly into oblivion.

She turned toward her husband and put her arms around him. The kiss they shared was more relief than romance.

By the time Jack got back to the gallery, the place was teeming with cops.

"Looks like Don got his man, I mean woman," said Smith, the first member of the police force to greet Jack.

"I didn't get anyone," Don said, hurrying over to them. "She shot herself."

"I still don't understand why she'd do that?" Jack said. "She was such a determined person who seemed to have every moment planned."

"I think she felt trapped. No way out and not wanting to face prosecution. She always put on a successful façade to the public, dressed well, excelled in everything she tried. I think she cared about her image," Jonathan said.

"Let's not forget, she was accused of a list of murders," Don said, "her father, her husband, Blondie and Silver Fox. Maybe there were others we don't even know about. And from what she told Nancy, she was very much alone and felt sad."

"It's hard to believe she felt anything," Jack said.

"She paid off my credit card debt for no apparent reason," Jonathan said.

"Well, that explains your odd allegiance to someone who was obsessed with killing me," Jack said.

"I think that's more out of character than her shooting herself," Don said. "Her mother committed suicide. Maybe it was in her genes."

While the three of them continued to double think Jill, the party raged on inside the gallery as if nothing had happened in the adjoining stairwell.

# Chapter 41

Caroline and Jack entered the office of McCurdy, Lundell, Strife and Roth in the Met Life building above Grand Central Station. They brought a mixture of curiosity and foreboding.

"We're here to see Alan Lundell," Caroline said, as she introduced herself to the receptionist. He had promised an unusual, though exciting turn of events concerning their daughter, Carrie. After much discussion, they decided to find out what this was all about. Despite Jack's protest, at the last minute Caroline invited her dad to join them.

The minute Lundell came out to greet them, a shriek escaped from Caroline's throat. The attorney pulled his extended hand away and stepped back, unsure of what caused such a distressing reaction from a woman he had never met.

"I've seen your face before," she said.

"Me too," Don said, as he entered the office.

"I don't mean to offend, but I don't recall meeting either of you," Lundell said, flashing a confident smile with teeth as white as his starched shirt that looked even brighter against his dark, perfectly tailored suit.

"I saw your face in a doll factory. Did you receive a doll that looks like you?" Caroline said.

Jack stared at his wife, then put his arm around her shoulder, a protective gesture.

"Why, yes, in fact I did. How do you know?"

"Jill gave it to you, right?"

"You mean Jessica. Recently she liked to use her twin sister's name. Jill died in an accident on the playground before the girls were in kindergarten."

"She had a twin!" Caroline and Jack said, gasping at the same time.

"Yes. The kids were taking turns pushing each other on the swings. Jill was the more fragile one, didn't hold on to the swings as tightly as she should. Jessica was more athletic, much stronger. She shoved so hard, her sister fell off and broke her neck. The family never fully recovered."

"Crazy from the start," Don said.

"I watched Jessica grow up, saw her morph into a very tough person," Lundell said, without acknowledging Don's comment. "She became my client after her father had an unfortunate fatal accident out west."

He moved his fingers through his hair, seeming to pause for effect.

"The doll she gave me is a great replica," Lundell said. "My kids love to tease me about it. My wife thinks it's sinister, so I brought it to my office. Come on in and I'll show it to you."

"This is the third potential victim Dad and I saw at the doll factory," Caroline said in a whisper to her husband. "This guy must have had sex with Jill. I want to get out of here."

233

"Let's at least hear what he has to say," Jack said, "then we can put this whole nightmare behind us and never have to mention the name Jill again."

"We have a rather surprising situation," Lundell said, once he was settled behind his mahogany desk. "Jessica perished without any next of kin. Her twin and her parents passed away before her, as did her husband. There are no living aunts, uncles or cousins. She led a rather lonesome life, as far as I can tell."

Caroline stared at the doll on a shelf behind Lundell and then at Lundell. The perfect reproduction made her shiver.

"Jessica's parents left her a multi-million-dollar house in Connecticut and a lot of money," Lundell said. "A fairly substantial sum."

"What does that have to do with my family?" Don said, taking over the conversation.

"Well," the attorney said, seeming to enjoy a delay delivering his news, "under normal circumstances, with no heirs, her entire estate would go to the state."

"So why are we here?" said Jack, trying not to sound confrontational.

"I'm getting to that. The good news is that Jessica was smart. Recently, she created a will."

Caroline and Jack looked at each other, taking deep breaths simultaneously.

"Jessica left her Porsche to Jonathan. I probably shouldn't tell you, but I think he works for you, right?"

"You're referring to the manager of my New York gallery," Jack said. "I knew they were friends. It bothered me that he seemed able to overlook her ominous side."

"Money can sometimes do that," the attorney said, while nodding.

Jack and Caroline kept quiet.

Then Lundell leaned back, creating more drama.

"Everything else goes to Carrie," he said, then waited for a reaction.

"No shit," Don said.

Caroline and Jack looked at each other, astounded.

"We don't want it," Jack said. "It's dirty money. Besides, Carrie is a twin. Whatever she inherits would have to be shared with her sister.

"Not according to the law," Lundell said, while Don muttered "schmuck" loud enough for Caroline to hear. "Before I explain what happens next, Jessica left a letter for Jack. With your permission, I'd like to read it to all of you."

Jack nodded, realizing he'd show it to Caroline and Don anyway.

*Dear Jack,*

*If you are reading this letter, I have died, probably violently considering all I've done. One good thing is that I fell in love. Not with you, with your daughter, Carrie, the one who reminds me of myself. I didn't know my heart was alive until she touched it. There's nobody else in my world to leave my money to. Help Carrie create a life filled with ice cream and good deeds. That's my plan.*

The attorney paused to take a breath.

"This letter is too nice. I don't believe Jill wrote it," Jack said.

Caroline grunted.

Lundell continued to read aloud.

*Before you relax, know that while I may be dead, I'm not going away. I'm not finished. As my father taught me, planning, patience, perfection.*

*Game over, or is it?*

*Jill*

"What the hell does that mean?" Jack said.

"It's a bit sinister, but I'd ignore the ending of her message," Lundell said. "Jessica was always tormenting people whenever she could. She's gone now. You'll probably want to sell her house and add the cash to the portfolio. The place is small compared to other homes in that neighborhood. You might only get $3 million."

"It's dirty money," Jack repeated. "A reward for misbehavior. How would I explain this to my kids?"

"Mr. Lundell," Caroline said, "I know why you received a look-alike doll. What would you do if you were her beneficiary?"

"Me? I shouldn't respond, but I have thought about it since drafting Jessica's will, even wish it were me. I'd take the money. Maybe give some to charity. I certainly wouldn't complain about it."

"We're not complaining," Jack said. "We're trying to understand. Exactly how much is involved, the estimated value of the house plus the stocks and cash?"

"Just over eleven million dollars."

Jack whistled.

"Go ahead, you can whistle again."

"Can the parents use any of the money before Carrie turns 18?" Don said. "What are the rules here?"

"The court will appoint a guardian to protect your child's financial interests while she's a minor. The money can be used to pay for her expenses, but not yours or her sister's," Lundell said, directly to Caroline and Jack. "That could include private schools, tutors, sports or music lessons, vacations, even a wedding though chances are she won't be walking down the aisle before she turns 18 and takes control of her fortune."

Don sat quietly, nodding his head.

"You need to meet her stockbroker. Unfortunately, Bill Turner, the man who advised Jessica and her father on all financial matters, was murdered recently or I would have included him in this meeting."

"Turner hired me to investigate Jill, or Jessica, just before he was killed. I called him Silver Fox," Don said.

"Someone at his firm is taking over and will manage Carrie's portfolio. I don't know who it is yet, but you can go there after our meeting. The company is in this building," Lundell said, handing Jack a phone number.

"Turner also received a look-alike doll," Caroline said. "You're very lucky Jill died before she got to you."

"Believe me, I'm well aware of all the extenuating circumstances," Lundell said. "As to the money, you have time, years, before any decisions need to be made. Your daughter has nine months after she comes of age to disclaim the will. I doubt that'll happen."

"We don't want the money," Jack said, again.

"It's not yours to reject," Lundell said." It's your daughter's, overseen by the court. Don't you understand, you have no say."

"And I want the money for Carrie," Caroline said, looking at her father.

Don got up, motioning Jack to follow him outside.

"Remember our conversation in London, Jack. I told you to make my daughter happy. That's what a father wants, right? Since you have no choice about accepting the inheritance right now, why not embrace it on behalf of Carrie. Both girls can share it when they come of age."

"If I have no say, then obviously Carrie gets the money, but I can't pretend to be happy about it."

"If you don't welcome this lucky twist of events, I'll let Caroline see the flash drive of you and Jill," Don said.

"So, you insist I pretend this is great, a façade I need to uphold for the next 11 years. You want me to act like all's well that ends well?" Jack said.

"Don't get Shakespearian on me."

Jack looked surprised.

"What?" said Don. "Just because I didn't go to an Ivy League college you think I don't read."

Jack stayed silent, shaking his head.

"Come on, get Caroline and let's go eat. You can buy me a Macallan neat to celebrate then put the whole lunch on my running tab."

"You don't have a running account with me."

"I do now," he said, removing a flash drive from his pocket and handing it to Jack. "We'll settle it on the twins' 18th birthday."

When Jack and Don returned to the attorney's office, Lundell was holding a package wrapped in brown paper.

"There's one more thing," he said. "Jessica left this for Carly."

Jack took the package and unwrapped it slowly. He opened the white box and removed white tissue paper. Inside was a miniature doll, a look-alike of Carly.

Caroline screamed.

"I have to...I have to...I have to..." Jack said, while his eyes twitched.

"Damn that fucking bitch," Don said, with clenched fists. If she weren't already dead, I'd kill her with my own hands."

"Relax," Lundell said. "The woman's dead. She can no longer hurt anyone. She got off on creating havoc and I think she was trying to extend her power over you psychologically. I'm not worried. Nor should you be."

When they left for lunch, they were arguing about how Carrie's new-found wealth would affect her relationship with her sister and the possibility that Jessica had hired Jonathan, or someone else, to complete her wishes for killing anyone who had received a doll.

\*\*\*\*

Two weeks later, the Greenwich newspapers carried a story about a local lawyer, Alan Lundell, who had been drugged then strangled with neon green shoelaces.

Marilyn Gottlieb began her writing career as a columnist for *Dan's Papers* on Long Island, New York. She was SVP, Director of Public Relations and a member of the 17-person Operations Committee for Lintas, a $1.8 billion worldwide advertising agency that was part of The Interpublic Group of Companies. Prior to that she was with Ogilvy & Mather and the American Association of Advertising Agencies. Inducted into the YWCA's prestigious Academy of Women Achievers, she also was an adjunct professor at the New School University and a member of the Board of Advertising Women of New York. Ms. Gottlieb attended Skidmore College and earned an MA from New York University and an MFA in Writing and Literature from Stony Brook Southampton. Her first book was *Life with an Accent* (2013). The young adult version came out in early 2016 and was published in Israel in Hebrew. Her novels include *Dance Me Younger* and the sequel, *Girl in the Wall. Beautiful Lunatic* is Ms. Gottlieb's fourth book.

Made in the USA
Middletown, DE
17 February 2022

61235092R00136